"Merrilee, are you afraid to be alone with me?" Grant asked.

"No!" Well…

"Good. I'll feed you and I want to show off since the last time you saw it."

If she continued to object, he might sense the reasons behind her reluctance, and her pride couldn't allow that, so she abandoned her protests. But she'd shut the door on a life with Grant long ago. Tonight she'd make certain it remained locked and barred.

As they neared Grant's place, her curiosity stirred. The one glimpse she'd had of the house that fateful summer years back had revealed a log cabin, ready to collapse in a strong wind. She'd hated the house the moment she saw it, but not liking the place had been the least of her problems that day.

The following morning she'd broken their engagement, certain she'd done the right thing. Even though she'd missed Grant terribly, she'd never doubted she'd made the best decision.

The last thing on earth she wanted was for Grant to prove her wrong.

Dear Reader,

To paraphrase an ancient Chinese saying, we live in
interesting times. Due to tumultuous world events,
we appreciate more than ever security, solace, acceptance
and love as bulwarks against the troubles of the day.
In my new series, A PLACE TO CALL HOME, I've created
a small town in upstate South Carolina where love and
acceptance, along with only the occasional mayhem,
abound. For the residents of Pleasant Valley, friends
are family, and family is everything.

In *Almost Heaven*, book one of the series, Merrilee Stratton
has fled Pleasant Valley for New York City to follow her
dream of becoming a famous photographer. When a
family crisis calls her home, she can't avoid her ex-fiancé,
Grant Nathan, a handsome country vet. Will Merrilee
come to realize that everything she's searched for has been
in Pleasant Valley all along—and that there's no place like
home?

I hope you enjoy Merrilee and Grant's story, and, as we
say in the South, y'all come back and visit Pleasant Valley
again in book two, *One Good Man*, will be out in January
2005.

Happy reading!

Charlotte Douglas

CHARLOTTE DOUGLAS
Almost Heaven

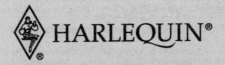

TORONTO • NEW YORK • LONDON
AMSTERDAM • PARIS • SYDNEY • HAMBURG
STOCKHOLM • ATHENS • TOKYO • MILAN • MADRID
PRAGUE • WARSAW • BUDAPEST • AUCKLAND

ISBN 0-373-75042-0

ALMOST HEAVEN

www.eHarlequin.com

Printed in U.S.A.

ABOUT THE AUTHOR

The major passions of Charlotte Douglas's life are her husband—her high school sweetheart to whom she's been married for over three decades—and writing compelling stories. A national bestselling author, she enjoys filling her books with love of home and family, special places and happy endings. With their two cairn terriers, she and her husband live most of the year on Florida's central west coast, but spend the warmer months at their North Carolina mountaintop retreat.

No matter what time of year, you can reach her at charlottedouglas1@juno.com. She's always delighted to hear from readers.

Books by Charlotte Douglas

HARLEQUIN AMERICAN ROMANCE

591—IT'S ABOUT TIME
623—BRINGING UP BABY
868—MONTANA MAIL-ORDER WIFE*
961—SURPRISE INHERITANCE
999—DR. WONDERFUL
1027—VERDICT: DADDY
1038—ALMOST HEAVEN†

HARLEQUIN INTRIGUE

380—DREAM MAKER
434—BEN'S WIFE
482—FIRST-CLASS FATHER
515—A WOMAN OF MYSTERY
536—UNDERCOVER DAD
611—STRANGER IN HIS ARMS*
638—LICENSED TO MARRY
668—MONTANA SECRETS
691—THE BRIDE'S RESCUER
740—THE CHRISTMAS TARGET

†A Place To Call Home
*Identity Swap

Chapter One

MJ Stratton hoisted the strap of her camera bag higher over her shoulder and wearily tackled the last flight of stairs to her fourth-floor apartment.

"First thing when I become rich and famous," she muttered with what little breath she had left, "I'm renting in a building with an elevator."

Unlocking her door, she consoled herself with the fact that at least her apartment had a comfortable bed, one she would hit as soon as she dumped her equipment. The wedding reception at the posh Manhattan hotel had lasted past 1:00 a.m., and the bride's mother had insisted that MJ snap candid shots until the final guest departed.

After entering the apartment, she secured the door behind her and flicked on the lights. With a sigh of relief, she slid her bulky camera bag into the closet and tossed her coat and hat on top of it. Kicking off her shoes and tugging off her blouse, she headed for the bedroom.

The wedding had been a royal pain. The bride had refused to be photographed from any angle except her left side, and the bride's mother had followed MJ like a Velcro shadow, attempting to dictate every picture's composition. Fortunately, MJ reassured herself, the hefty fee from the annoying assignment would pay her bills until she lined up more work.

If all else failed, the job at the gallery was still open. Maybe she should just take it. She'd engaged in this argument with herself before and, as always, ended up admitting she'd have more money with a steady job but even less time for her own art. She'd arrived in New York six years ago expecting to make a big splash with her photographs, but so far she had yet to produce a ripple.

Weariness consumed her. After pulling on the oversize T-shirt she used as a nightgown, she crawled between the covers and switched off the lamp. She would have dropped instantly to sleep, except for the insistent flashing of a small red light, indicating a message on the answering machine on her bedside table. She turned onto her other side and pulled the pillow over her head to block the annoying blinking. The message could wait until morning.

It is already morning, she thought with an exhausted sigh, but no point in listening to the message now. Whoever had left it had probably long since gone to bed.

MJ closed her eyes, but sleep wouldn't come. The waiting message stirred her curiosity. What if it was her big break, a call from a gallery that had seen her work and wanted to exhibit her photographs? Or an offer for another job, photographing a Bar Mitzvah or a lavish children's party with income that would keep her solvent into next month? Unable to sleep without knowing, she rolled over, flipped on the light and pressed Play.

"Hello, Merrilee June." The soft, cultured drawl of her grandmother filled the room, but a sense of urgency tinged its usual calm. "We have a family emergency and I need you at home right away. I've reserved you a seat on the 7:00 a.m. flight out of JFK into Greenville. See you soon."

"End of message," the machine announced.

Heart pounding, MJ bolted upright in bed. "That's it?" she yelled at the machine. "You aren't going to tell me what's wrong?"

Adrenaline surged through her veins. Sleep was impossible with a dozen dire possibilities flitting through her mind. She grabbed the phone and dialed her grandmother's number. After waiting more than twelve rings, she had no answer. Her nana, Sally Mae McDonough, apparently still persisted in her lifelong habit of unplugging her phone when she went to bed.

"If it's bad news, I'd rather hear it in the morning,"

Nana had always insisted. "And if it's urgent, the police will come to the house and wake me."

Bad news?

MJ's heart raced. Had Nana, sticking to her own philosophy, decided to spare MJ the unhappy details until daylight?

Lacking her grandmother's stoicism, MJ dialed her parents' home. She wanted to hear their voices to assure herself that Jim and Cat Stratton were all right. After four rings, her mother's voice mail kicked in. MJ tried three times with the same results.

At each unanswered call, her panic grew. With trembling fingers, she punched in the number of her father's veterinary clinic. Again she reached only voice mail with a message to call Dr. Grant Nathan, her father's partner, in case of an emergency.

Desperate to discover what crisis had precipitated her grandmother's cryptic message, MJ tried Information.

"What city?" the computerized voice asked.

"Pleasant Valley, South Carolina."

"What listing?"

"The Pleasant Valley Police Department."

The artificial voice rattled off a number. MJ scribbled it hastily, then punched it in.

"Police Department," a familiar female voice answered. "Officer Sawyer speaking."

"Brynn! Thank God, I'm actually talking to a live person," MJ said.

"Merrilee? Are you in town?" her old high school friend asked.

MJ pictured Brynn, short red curls, intense, dark blue eyes, her slender but curvy figure doing things for a police uniform no male body ever could. Guys in Pleasant Valley had been known to break speed limits just for an encounter with the beautiful Officer Sawyer. Not that it ever did them any good. Brynn was married to her job.

"I'm in New York," MJ explained. "I had a message from Nana about a family emergency, but she didn't say what it is. I'm frantic and can't reach anyone. Do you know if my folks are okay?"

A dead silence on the other end of the line intensified MJ's fears. "Brynn? Are you still there?"

"Your folks are fine, as far as I'm aware," Brynn answered in a tone that indicated she knew more than she was telling. "I saw your dad and grandmother earlier tonight before I came to work."

"And my mom?"

"She's taking classes at the university in Asheville. Sometimes she stays over if she's working late in the library."

MJ wasn't surprised that Brynn knew her mother's schedule. In the small town of Pleasant Valley, everyone knew everybody else's business, one of the many reasons MJ had moved away immediately after her graduation from college.

A chilling thought struck her. "What if there's been an accident?"

"I would have heard about a traffic accident through our dispatcher," Brynn assured her. "Look, if it makes you feel better, I can call the local hospitals and check to see if either of your parents or your grandmother has been admitted."

"Would you?" MJ remembered what six years in the big city had caused her to forget. Brynn had always bent over backward to help people. Her willingness to be of assistance was one of many factors that made her a good cop. And a terrific friend.

"Give me your number," Brynn said, "and I'll call you back as soon as I've checked."

MJ rattled off her number, thanked her old friend and hung up. Sleep was impossible now, so she might as well pack. She'd have to leave for the airport soon anyway.

With cold dread weighting her heart, she tossed clothes into her suitcase. She was zipping the lid when the phone rang.

"It's Brynn," her friend said when MJ answered. "I checked the local hospitals. No admissions for any of your folks."

"Thanks, Brynn. I owe you."

MJ replaced the receiver in its cradle. Brynn's news gave her little reassurance. If a member of MJ's family had suffered an illness or injury serious enough to require a trauma unit, they'd have been transported to the Greenville hospital. Or her mother could be hospitalized in Asheville.

MJ tugged on the clothes she'd removed earlier and called a cab. Anxiety overrode her anger toward Nana for leaving such a cryptic message. In just a few hours MJ would be in Pleasant Valley again. For the first time since she had left after college, she was actually looking forward to returning to the boring, sleepy little town, if only to settle her fears.

EXHAUSTION temporarily overcame her foreboding. The flight attendant's voice, announcing their imminent arrival in Greenville, awoke MJ. With consciousness, her anxiety returned in a rush.

As soon as the plane taxied to a stop, MJ grabbed her camera bag from the overhead compartment and headed for the exit. Within minutes she was striding across the concourse toward the baggage carousels.

Suddenly strong hands grasped her shoulders from behind and swung her around.

"Merrilee June. Long time, no see." The rich, deep voice initiated a cascade of memories, all pleasurable; ones she'd worked hard to forget.

She glanced up at Grant Nathan, who'd intercepted her. If bad luck came in bundles, here was walking proof. For six years she'd managed to avoid him, had worked hard to push him from her mind. Now she tried to stop the corresponding flutter of her heart. She might as well have attempted to stop its beating.

If anything, the vet was even more attractive than she'd remembered, exuding enough self-confidence and masculinity to make any woman's heart stutter. She'd forgotten how tall he was, well over six feet, and his practice as a country vet, tramping through fields, lifting small animals and maneuvering cows and horses for treatment, had given him a physique few personal trainers could replicate. In spite of her efforts not to, she remembered too well how many times she'd nestled her head against those broad shoulders and how comforting the embrace of his strong arms had been.

Six years had added a maturity that sat well on the strong planes of his tanned face. Tiny lines from laughter and squinting in the bright sun framed bourbon-brown eyes flecked with gold. A few premature strands of gray, threaded through his thick honey-colored hair at the temples, were the only visible signs of his thirty-four years. His dimpled grin displayed the same boyish charm and reminded MJ too well of the many times those lips had kissed hers.

She shoved aside the memories, whose pull had been

both the driving force and the toughest part of her decision to leave Pleasant Valley for good. "What are you doing here, Grant? Taking a trip?"

He held her by the shoulders with strong but gentle hands, and his gaze searched her face, as if in assessment. "I'm on an errand of mercy. Your grandmother sent me to pick you up."

MJ wiggled from his grasp before she succumbed to the desire to snuggle against him, as she had so often in the old days. Those times were gone forever. "You've wasted a trip. I'm renting a car."

"Mrs. McDonough said there's no need. And she doesn't want you driving while you're agitated."

MJ's temper soared. "I'd be a lot less agitated if I knew what the hell is going on." Already worried sick about her folks, she resented having to struggle with old feelings for Grant Nathan, too. "Besides, I'll need a car of my own, so you might as well leave."

Grant shook his head. "You grandmother said you can use hers. She doesn't drive much these days."

MJ's breath caught in her throat. "Nana's all right?"

"Feisty as ever," Grant said with a grin.

"Then what's the family emergency she called me about?" Her anger flared again, and a sneaking suspicion kicked in. "This isn't just a ploy to lure me home, is it?"

MJ wouldn't put it past Nana to play at matchmaking, but surely even her persistent grandmother recognized that what MJ had shared with Grant was long over.

Grant's expression sobered. He glanced across the concourse as if to avoid her gaze. "I don't know if *emergency* is the word I'd use, but you're definitely needed here."

MJ's knees went weak and she sank onto the nearest seat. "My mom? Dad? Are they okay?"

"They're not sick or injured, if that's what you're asking." Again he evaded her eyes.

"But they're okay?" she insisted.

Grant looked ill at ease. "I promised your grandmother I'd let her fill you in."

MJ crossed her arms over her chest and set her jaw. "I've been up all night, I'm worried out of my mind, and I'm not going anywhere until you tell me what's wrong. Something *is* wrong, isn't it?"

"Merrilee June—"

"I'm MJ now."

Grant's eyebrows lifted in surprise. "Why?"

"So I don't sound like a character from *Gone With the Wind,*" MJ said irritably. "Now, are you going to tell me what's wrong or not?"

"MJ," Grant said with a grimace, as if the nickname left a bad taste in his mouth, "you know I won't go back on my word to your grandmother."

"A thousand horrible possibilities are driving me crazy! Don't you feel any loyalty to me?"

His expression darkened. "As I recall, you cut me loose from any obligation six years ago."

MJ's panic meter was registering overload. She grabbed Grant by the biceps and attempted to shake him. She might as well have tried to move a tree. "Then for old times' sake, please tell me what's wrong."

Her voice, loud and frantic, traveled across the concourse, drawing stares from other travelers.

"Calm down, Merrilee June, or I'll have to go to my truck for horse tranquilizers."

"Calm down!" Her voice rose an octave. "How calm would you be in my place?"

"The sooner we get going, the sooner your grandmother can fill you in," Grant said, so reasonably she wanted to hit him. "I've already told you it's not a life-and-death matter. Cat and Jim couldn't be healthier. Sally Mae will explain the rest."

Admitting defeat, MJ released her grip. She'd forgotten how stubborn Grant could be. Not actually forgotten, she realized. She'd simply relegated everything about him to the back of her mind. When she'd first moved to New York, that tactic was the only way she'd survived missing him.

"Is that all your luggage?" Grant nodded toward her camera bag.

MJ shook her head. "I have another bag. I didn't know how long I'd have to stay. Still don't," she said accusingly, "since I haven't a clue why I'm here in the first place."

Grant grasped her elbow and steered her toward the baggage claim area. "I'm not breaking my promise to Sally Mae by admitting you'll be here a good while."

"A week?" MJ prodded.

"Probably longer," Grant said, "but, hey, it's springtime in Pleasant Valley. You might as well enjoy it."

At Grant's easy manner, MJ's anxiety lessened slightly. As her father's business partner, Grant was fond of both her parents. If they were in imminent danger, he wouldn't be so relaxed. Intense curiosity replaced her fears. What in heaven's name was going on that would make Nana call her home from New York in the middle of the night? And how serious was the situation that solving it could take weeks?

MJ quickened her steps. Nana had a lot of explaining to do.

MJ parted with Grant at the baggage carousel and waited for her luggage while he went for his truck. When she picked up her bag, exited the airport and found him parked at curbside, her heart did flip-flops. The pickup was new, but the same make and color as the truck he'd had six years ago.

The years melted away and she was a college student again, home for spring break and waiting for Grant to arrive at her parents' house. She'd known Grant all her life. He was six years older, but MJ had been best friends with his sister Jodie. The Nathans lived around the block from the Strattons, their backyards adjoined, and MJ and Jodie had been inseparable as children, even though Jodie had been two grades ahead of MJ in school. For MJ, an only child, Jodie had been the sister she'd always wanted. And Grant had been the handsome big brother, one who couldn't be bothered with "the DTs," short for Double Trouble, as he'd called MJ and Jodie.

The summer before MJ's senior year in college, everything had changed.

Until that summer, she hadn't seen much of Grant for years. First, he'd gone away to college, then veterinary school, and finally to an internship at an animal clinic in Georgia. Jodie had kept MJ informed of her brother's activities in her letters to MJ at school, but MJ, busy with college courses and new friends, hadn't given much thought to the boy she'd had a crush on through elementary and high school.

The summer after her junior year, her parents had welcomed her home with such enthusiasm that MJ again experienced momentary guilt at choosing a college in California that had kept her so far away. After only a few hours with her mother and father, however, her guilt had dissipated. Cat and Jim Stratton, even after more than two decades of marriage, were obviously crazy in love and the best of friends, as well. Merrilee June, as she'd called herself then, had recognized that when she eventually left home for good, her parents would miss her daily presence, but as long as they had each other, their lives would be complete.

"We're having company for dinner," her mother had announced upon Merrilee's return from college for the summer. "Your father's new partner."

Merrilee had rounded on her father with concern. "A partner? You're not slowing down?"

Jim Stratton had been in his late forties, which, to Merrilee, had seemed ancient at the time.

"On the contrary," her father had said with that amiable grin she adored. With his dark brown hair and soft gray eyes, Merrilee had always thought him the most handsome man in the world. No wonder her mother loved him so much.

"The practice is growing so fast," her father had explained, "I need all the help I can get. I've been working weekends for too long. I want to spend more time with your mother."

Cat had winked at her daughter. "What he really means is he's missing too many ball games on his brand-new, big-screen TV."

But Merrilee had known better. Her parents had always enjoyed activities together: hiking, white-water rafting and picnics in the nearby Smoky Mountains, tending the vegetable garden that consumed most of the backyard and driving to Greenville or Asheville to attend concerts. For as long as Merrilee could remember, her parents had loved playing records from the fifties and sixties and dancing something they called "the Shag" with the furniture pushed aside in the family room. The snappy and sensuous movements of the dance had caused electricity to crackle between them. And when her father did watch sports on TV, her mother was right beside him, engrossed in the game and yelling caustic comments at the officials, just like one of the guys. Her dad had jokingly bought her mother a rubber-foam brick she could throw at the umpires and not damage the screen.

Another favorite sport of Jim Stratton's was the opportunity to introduce his wife to someone new.

"Cat?" the person would usually ask. "Is that short for Catherine?"

Her mother would shake her head. "For Catawba. It's the name of the river near Rock Hill where my father grew up. He loved the river and the name, so I was stuck with Catawba."

Jim Stratton's eyes would twinkle with delight. "Good thing her dad didn't live on the river near Asheville. Instead of having a wife named Catawba, I'd have a French Broad," he'd explain with a satisfied chuckle and suggestive leer.

"Jim, please!" Cat's response was always indignant, but her soft blush and the gleam in her eye revealed that her mother actually loved her father's teasing.

For most of her life, all Merrilee had ever wanted was a man who'd love her like her father loved her mother. Although she'd worried that she'd never find a love as perfect as her parents', she'd still expected to marry, raise her children in Pleasant Valley and spend the rest of her life there.

But fate had other plans. When Merrilee chose to study fine arts at the University of California, her life changed forever. Aside from the occasional trip to Atlanta and family vacations to Florida, Merrilee had spent all her life in the town where she was born. California was culture shock.

"You wouldn't believe this place," she'd written Jodie. "It's totally different from the isolation of our ultraconservative Pleasant Valley. I've met people on campus from all over the world, and on weekends and holidays, I've traveled from San Diego to Monterey. The art museums, the restaurants, the theaters are incredible! And the people talk about philosophy, politics and all kinds of things, not just which restaurant makes the best barbecue or who's pregnant. Sometimes, Jodie, I swear, I don't ever want to come home."

With her college experiences, Merrilee's expectations had shifted. A love like her parents' would be nice, but only if her husband took her out of Pleasant Valley and gave her free rein to follow her career dreams and to travel the world. The prospect of settling down in the sleepy little town, which had once seemed idyllic, had seemed more like a death sentence.

Merrilee had been determined that the summer after her junior year would be the last she'd ever spend in Pleasant Valley.

Little had she guessed that fate was about to throw another curve in the form of her father's guest for dinner that night.

"So who is this new partner?" Merrilee had asked.

"It's a surprise," her mother had said with a glimmer in her blue eyes, exactly like Merrilee's.

And Merrilee had been surprised, all right. Not so much by the fact that her father's partner was Grant Nathan as by Grant's effect on her. When he'd entered the Stratton living room that night, Merrilee's teenage crush had enveloped her in an overwhelming rush that metamorphosed into something much stronger and more breathtaking.

Merrilee had fallen in love.

And from the corresponding gleam in Grant's eyes, she'd guessed correctly that he'd experienced the same emotion.

That was then, this is now, she reminded herself as they drove further upstate through the foothills of South Carolina toward the mountains. She shoved the memories and the emotions they evoked into that deep compartment of her heart where she'd kept them locked away these past several years. She'd severed her connection to Grant six years ago. For good. No need to revisit dead dreams.

But Grant's presence, the steady, even sound of his breathing, his striking profile and distinctive male scent, and the easy manner with which his strong, capable fingers gripped the steering wheel, made slamming the door on those feelings again harder than when he'd been six hundred miles away.

To distract her attention from the enticing man at her side, MJ gazed out the window. Her sojourn in New York City had made her forget the beauty of South Carolina in early spring. In almost every yard, Bradford pear trees in full bloom reminded her of billowing bridal dresses. Arching branches of forsythia in vibrant yellow and stalks of brilliant purple irises provided splashes of color against the bright green of new grass, all framed against a cloudless sky of startling blue.

The highway soon left the towns and fields of the foothills and ascended into mountain forests, where an occasional clearing revealed ridge after ridge of the Smoky Mountains to the northwest, the deep emerald of their gentle folds and high peaks in stark contrast against the clear sky. MJ's fingers itched for her camera, packed in its bag behind her seat.

With the familiar farms, small towns and forests unchanged and Grant once again beside her, MJ traveled through the countryside as if the intervening six years had never happened.

But they had.

She had left Pleasant Valley for good, with the exception of a rare holiday visit, and she had permanently cut all ties with Grant. If not for her parents and Nana, MJ would never have returned to the small town where she'd grown up. Unlike the smorgasbord of cultural and recreational delights of New York and its myriad opportunities for an aspiring artist, Pleasant Valley had nothing to offer except dead ends.

But in spite of MJ's resolve to put the past behind her, coming home affected her. The sight of the white Colonial-style Welcome sign at the town limits brought an unexpected lump to her throat. After crossing the bridge over the river that paralleled Piedmont Avenue, the main thoroughfare, she found herself leaning forward, eager for her first glimpse of her grandmother's impressive two-story house with its white clapboards and wide wraparound porch, only a block from downtown.

Nana must have been watching the street, because as soon as Grant pulled to the curb, the front door with its leaded-glass panes opened and Sally Mae McDonough stepped onto the porch. Dressed in a simple navy dress and matching low-heeled pumps, pearls at her throat and ears, and her white hair elegantly styled, Nana hadn't changed since MJ's last visit a year ago Christmas. Slender with perfect posture, her grandmother remained the quintessential Southern belle.

In other words, MJ thought with an inward grin, a steamroller disguised as a powder puff.

After seeing her Nana unchanged, MJ exhaled a sigh of relief. Nana, at least, as Grant had promised, seemed fine.

With a camel-colored cashmere cardigan draped around her shoulders, Nana waited until MJ climbed the stairs before speaking.

"Welcome home, child. It's been too long."

MJ hugged her grandmother, breathed in her signature scent of lilacs and reveled in the warmth of the familiar embrace. "It's good to see you, Nana."

"We missed you at Christmas."

MJ fought rising guilt. "You know I had to work. I photographed seven weddings over the holidays."

Her earnings had given her a precious few weeks off in January, time to add to her portfolio of the faces and places of the city in preparation for an exhibit of her own someday.

MJ lived for that someday.

"Wait!" Nana, who seldom raised her voice, had spoken loudly to Grant, who was still at the curb. "Is Gloria with you?"

"No, ma'am," Grant replied. "She's at home. And none too happy about it, either."

Nana's relief was evident. And MJ's curiosity blossomed. Gloria? Jodie's latest letters had said nothing about her brother's girlfriend. An uncomfortable sensation settled over MJ and she shrugged it off. She was beyond jealousy. After all, she'd ended her relationship with Grant long ago when things hadn't worked out as she'd hoped. She was actually surprised he hadn't married and had children by now, but she didn't stop to analyze why such a prospect annoyed her.

"You can set the bags in the front hall," Nana said to Grant, who had followed MJ up the walk.

Nana held open the door and MJ and Grant stepped inside.

"Here she is, safe and sound, like I promised," Grant announced, "so I'll be on my way. Gloria's not happy when I'm away too long."

MJ couldn't picture Grant with a clinging vine type. He'd evidently changed a great deal in the past six years. She gave herself an inward shake. She didn't need the distraction of an old relationship now and was glad he was leaving. But her relief at his impending departure was short-lived.

"You're not going now," Nana said in her soft drawl with its underlying hint of steel that defied contradiction. "I know you had breakfast at 5:00 a.m., as usual, and it's almost noon. I have lunch ready in the dining room. We can talk as we eat."

"This is family business," Grant said, apparently anxious to return to Gloria. "I don't want to intrude."

"Fiddlesticks," Nana said. "You're Jim's partner. That makes you family. Besides, I need your help."

MJ watched with undisguised amusement as Grant relented. Not even his strong will could refuse the command in Nana's tone. He followed Sally Mae into the dining room and pulled out a chair for her at the head of the table. MJ sat on her grandmother's right. Grant took a chair at Nana's left, looking as if he were attending his own execution.

Nana reached for the silver pitcher in front of her place. "Iced tea?"

MJ's nerves had reached their breaking point. "This isn't a social event, Nana. I want to know what's wrong, and I want to know *now*."

Her grandmother set the pitcher down with a thud and for a fleeting instant looked as if she were going to cry, something MJ had never witnessed in her twenty-eight years, not even the night her grandfather had died.

MJ held her breath as, with apparent Herculean effort, Sally Mae regained her composure and spoke so softly, MJ strained to hear.

"Your father," her grandmother said in a voice without inflection, "has left your mother."

Chapter Two

Grant's reaction to Merrilee's dilemma surprised him. He drew on all his self-control to keep from rising and going to her. Touched by the distress on her face, he craved to pull her into his arms and to comfort her. But she hadn't wanted him six years ago and she sure as hell didn't want him now, especially when her world had just caved in.

Irritation at his inadequacy consumed him. He could calm a raging bull, soothe a four-hundred-pound sow with blood in her eye, pacify a wild stallion and handle wild-eyed feral cats. But today, just like six years ago, he was helpless to communicate with, must less console, one small but incredibly beautiful and desirable woman.

"Daddy left?" Merrilee's face had gone white, her eyes, the color of a Carolina mountain sky, had widened with shock and, for an instant, Grant feared she would faint. "What do you mean?"

Sally Mae's aristocratic features twisted into a wry

grimace. "You may have spent the last few years among Yankees, but surely you still understand plain English. *Left* means exactly what it says."

"He's moved out?" Merrilee looked as if she was having trouble breathing.

Grant fought the impulse to close his eyes against her distress.

"In a word, yes," her grandmother replied.

For Merrilee's sake, Grant wished Sally Mae hadn't been so blunt, but he didn't know how else she could have broken such unpleasant news except straight-out.

"Why?" Merrilee insisted.

Grant clamped his jaw to keep from interfering. Working day-in and day-out with Jim Stratton, Grant had witnessed the transformation in his partner and friend, but informing Merrilee was Sally Mae's responsibility. Grant just hoped the older woman would break the details more gently.

"It's a long story," Sally Mae said.

"This has been going on for a while?" Merrilee's face flushed, color returning with her anger. "Why didn't anyone let me know?"

"Things didn't come to a head until yesterday." Her grandmother's grim expression added years to her appearance. "No one thought Jim would go that far."

That much was true, Grant thought. He'd believed his partner's foolish actions a temporary aberration. He'd never guessed that Jim would take such drastic measures.

"What about Mom? Is she okay?"

"I haven't spoken with your mother for several days," Sally Mae said. "She's staying at her apartment in Asheville."

"Her apartment?" Merrilee's confusion was evident. "I thought you said Dad moved out."

Sally Mae took a deep breath, the only outward sign she was struggling for control. "I'd better start at the beginning. Last summer, your father started putting in long hours, pushing himself too hard. He seldom slept or took time to eat."

MJ turned an accusing glance on Grant. "I thought you were supposed to help him. Isn't that what a partner's for?"

"We've both been up to our necks." Grant met her gaze and, although her anger stung, refused to take it personally. His conscience was clear. "Old Doc Gregory over in Walhalla died. Jim and I have been taking up the slack until a new vet takes over his practice."

"Are you telling me Dad's lost his mind from working too hard?" Merrilee asked her grandmother.

"Oh, Jim's not crazy," Sally Mae said quickly. "But overwork, sleep deprivation, lack of good nutrition, and the realization he's not getting any younger have left his judgment impaired."

Merrilee shook her head and a strand of hair the color of sunshine on corn silk fell over one eye. Grant squelched the urge to reach across the table to push it back. Merrilee had made it clear long ago she didn't want his touch.

After the way she'd dumped him so abruptly, had refused to answer his phone calls or letters, had acted as if he'd dropped off the face of the earth, had caused him endless sleepless nights and heartache, Grant should take satisfaction at her distress.

But he didn't.

He couldn't.

All he wanted was to make her world right for her again, something he couldn't do with Jim Stratton off the rails and acting crazy.

"Mom usually watches Dad like a hawk," Merrilee said, "to make sure he takes care of himself. She wouldn't have let this happen."

The glaze of shock had returned to her amazing blue eyes and Grant's old pull toward her tightened again, tugging on his heartstrings.

"Your mother's been preoccupied," Sally Mae said.

"With teaching?" Merrilee shook her head. "Mom never put her career first. Dad's always been the center of her universe."

"Her universe has shifted," Sally Mae said with dry disapproval. "Cat took a sabbatical last fall. Went back to school for her Ph.D."

"I know that," Merrilee said. "I may not have come home, but I have stayed in touch by phone and e-mail."

"And your parents have told you only what they wanted you to know," her grandmother said sharply. Sally Mae's expression and her voice softened. "Don't blame yourself. None of us knew the full extent of the problem. Not until yesterday."

Merrilee straightened her shoulders, as if bearing up under a heavy burden. "So you're telling me, with Dad's heavy workload and midlife crisis and Mom's going back to school, my parents have simply drifted apart?"

Sally Mae nodded, and Grant kept quiet, waiting for the bomb to drop.

"No wonder you called me," Merrilee said with a sigh that sounded relieved. "I'll talk to them. I know how much they love each other. If I can get them to communicate, they can work this out."

Grant closed his eyes. *Here it comes.*

Sally Mae fidgeted with the sterling silver flatware beside her plate. "There's a…complication."

"What kind of complication?" Merrilee didn't have a clue and Grant wished she could remain ignorant. The truth was going to break her heart.

"Ginger Parker," Sally Mae said in a tone that suggested the mere name made her sick to her stomach. "She's the complication."

"Another woman?" Merrilee said with a gasp, as if someone had sucker-punched her. "My dad with another woman? I don't believe it!"

"That's where he went when he moved out," her grandmother said with obvious distaste. "There's no fool like an old fool."

"Who is this Ginger?" Merrilee demanded. "I've never heard of her."

"Tell her, please, Grant," Sally Mae said. "Just talking about that…that *woman* makes me ill."

From the emphasis Sally Mae gave the word, Grant knew full well *woman* wasn't what Merrilee's grandmother had in mind, but she was too well-bred to verbalize her true opinion. Grant could think of a dozen words that fit Ginger Parker, but none that would ever cross Sally Mae McDonough's lips.

Merrilee's gaze fixed on him, waiting.

"Mrs. Parker came here over a year ago," he began. "She bought the old Patterson place up on Cradle Creek."

"'Mrs.'? She's married?" Merrilee asked in a tone even more horrified than before.

"A widow," Grant explained. "Moved here from New Jersey when her husband died."

"What does she look like?" Merrilee said. "Young and pretty, I'll bet."

"Bottle pretty," Sally Mae said with a sniff. "She

must spend a small fortune on auburn hair dye. And applies her makeup with a trowel. Amy Lou down at the Hair Apparent has made enough profit off that woman to buy a new car."

"Mrs. Parker is several years older than your father," Grant added.

Merrilee's mouth gaped. "Daddy left Mom for an *older* woman? I don't believe it."

"She may be older, but she keeps herself in shape," Grant said. "She's a runner. Jogs for miles every day in tight little spandex outfits that accent her behind and, uh, generous chest size." Grant glanced at Sally Mae, whose eyes were closed in disgust. "And she chooses her routes carefully."

"Chooses her routes?" Merrilee frowned.

"Her jogging itinerary makes her highly visible to the male population," Grant explained. "The woman's been hot to trot ever since she arrived in Pleasant Valley. She's cast her net at every man in town."

"Correction," Sally Mae interjected, "only at men with money. She's a gold digger."

"Unfortunately," Grant said, "your father's the first catch she's landed."

"The others had more sense," Sally Mae said with distinct bitterness.

Grant didn't bother mentioning how Ginger Parker had made a play for him last fall, pretending to sprain her ankle in front of his house. When he'd picked her up off the driveway, she'd twined her arms around his neck, pressed her breasts against his chest, batted her eyelashes and asked him to take her home. She'd filled his ear the whole time with how lonely she'd been since her husband, a retired army colonel, had died, and had shed tears that seemed transparently fake.

Refusing to fall for her ploy, Grant had called 9-1-1, and Brynn Sawyer had driven the woman to the hospital in her patrol car. After a thorough examination and X rays, the ER doctor had found nothing wrong with Ginger's ankle and sent her home. Jim Stratton may have found the woman sexy, but Grant thought her pathetic.

Guilt gnawed at Grant. Ginger had been as persistent as a burr on a dog. She'd bought a canary after the twisted ankle encounter and showed up at the clinic for a consultation. If Grant hadn't pawned her off on Jim, believing her no danger to his happily married partner, maybe none of this would have happened.

Merrilee shook her head. "I can't believe this. Daddy has more sense than to fall for another woman, much less one like that."

"Your father isn't thinking with his brain," Sally Mae said.

"Nana!" Merrilee's face flushed deep crimson.

Grant wasn't shocked by the oblique reference, only

that a woman as genteel as Sally Mae would utter it. What she'd said was true. Jim Stratton hadn't been thinking clearly for a long time. Ginger Parker had only one thing to offer a man like Jim.

Sex.

The two had nothing else in common.

"I'll talk to him," Merrilee said. "Make him see what a fool he's making of himself. And how much he's hurting Mom."

"No." Sally Mae shook her head firmly. "I don't think you should do that."

The older woman's response surprised Grant. He'd figured Sally Mae had summoned Merrilee home specifically to talk some sense into Jim. She was the apple of her father's eye and had always been able to wrap him around her little finger. Grant, too, before she shook the dust of Pleasant Valley off her shoes.

"Then why did you call me home?" Merrilee pushed back from the table, stood and paced the antique Oriental rug that covered the highly polished heart-pine floor.

"Men are stubborn," Sally Mae said. "The more you tell them they *shouldn't* do something, the more dead set they are to do it."

Grant opened his mouth to protest, but Sally Mae cut him off. "Sorry, Grant, but that's the truth as I see it, and especially where my son-in-law's concerned."

"If Daddy can't be influenced, what can I do?" Merrilee's reddened cheeks would have been appealing if not for her distress.

Sally Mae smiled with an almost feline cunning that made Grant glad she was plotting against Jim and not him. "I didn't say your father can't be influenced."

Merrilee took her seat. "I know that look, Nana. You've got something up your sleeve."

"Sit down, Merrilee June." Sally Mae reached for a platter of sandwiches and passed it to Grant. "You might as well eat while we talk. You're going to need your strength."

Grant was so hungry he didn't object to the dainty tuna salad sandwiches with the crusts removed. He filled his plate, but Merrilee took only half a sandwich and picked at it before taking a small bite.

"I want you to move back home," Sally Mae announced to her granddaughter.

Merrilee choked.

Grant raised his eyebrows. Merrilee had made her happiness at leaving Pleasant Valley abundantly clear, and nothing, not even Grant's marriage proposal, had been able to keep her here.

"You're not serious," Merrilee insisted once she'd cleared her throat.

"If you want to save your parents' marriage," Sally Mae said, "you must stay here. You can't help them long distance."

"If I can't talk to Dad, what good is staying?"

She had a point, Grant conceded, but he also was well aware that Sally Mae McDonough was one sharp cookie. She wouldn't have summoned Merrilee home without a specific plan.

Sally Mae patted her lips with a damask napkin and laid it beside her plate. "I said you shouldn't talk to him about *that woman.*"

Grant winced. On Sally Mae's lips, those two simple words sounded like the vilest profanity.

Merrilee cast her glance toward the ceiling as if seeking divine intervention. "Then what am I supposed to discuss? Cows and horses?"

Sally Mae's sly smile returned. "In a manner of speaking."

"What good would that do? Nana, I have my work in New York. I can't just move home and abandon it."

Sally Mae straightened her back, the proverbial steel magnolia. But her granddaughter was no slouch in the intestinal fortitude department, either. Grant waited, curious who would win this battle of wills.

Sally Mae nodded toward the hall, where Merrilee's bags sat. "You brought your camera. You can work here."

"There are precious few weddings in Pleasant Valley," Merrilee protested.

"And no Bar Mitzvahs," Grant added. Jim had kept

him informed on how Merrilee was earning her living in New York.

Merrilee shot him a grateful glance. "I can't support myself here."

"You won't have to," Sally Mae said. "I—"

"I won't accept charity," Merrilee said with a fierceness Grant remembered well. "When I left home, I vowed to make it on my own. I don't intend to return with my tail between my legs and my hand out."

With a sigh, Grant recalled that one of the things he'd loved most about Merrilee was her spunk. Without that gumption, she wouldn't have set out on her own. She wouldn't have left Pleasant Valley.

And him.

"I'm not giving any handouts," Sally Mae said. "I want to commission your work."

Merrilee's jaw dropped. "You want me to photograph you?"

"Lord, no," Sally Mae replied emphatically. "This old ruin doesn't need chronicling. I want to commission a book."

After Jim's infidelity, Grant had believed himself past surprising, but Sally Mae's proposal stunned him. What kind of book would interest a woman of her age and social standing? Merrilee's very pretty mouth was gaping again. Her grandmother's pronouncement had clearly left her speechless.

"I want you to record a pictorial account of the life of a country vet," Sally Mae said. "Dr. Jim Stratton, D.V.M. I'll pay all your expenses and underwrite its publication. It will make a stunning addition to your portfolio."

Merrilee shook her head. "I don't know. I'm not into pastoral settings. I prefer cityscapes."

Grant, however, saw immediately the tack Sally Mae was suggesting. "It's brilliant, Merrilee. You'll have to spend hours with your father, shooting him at work. The more you're with him, the better chance you have of bringing him back to reality. You'll be a constant reminder of what he's giving up."

"And," Sally Mae continued, "if you're living at home, you'll be a comfort to your mother. This…" She struggled for words. "This *foolishness* has to be breaking her heart."

"Mom has you to lean on," Merrilee said, but Grant could tell she was wavering.

"I will be here for your mother," Sally Mae said, "but I can't help your parents as you can. Every time your father looks at you, he'll see your resemblance to your mother, reminding him of his marriage and the happiness it's brought him. Heaven knows, he needs something to counteract the lust that's driving him."

"Lust!" Merrilee protested. "Dad's over fifty!"

"Over fifty but not dead," Sally Mae said with a wry smile. Her smile faded and her eyes grew flinty. "Although if you can't bring him to his senses, I might have to rectify that."

"Your grandmother's plan has merit." Grant struggled to remain objective. He had motives of his own, besides his friendship with Jim Stratton, for wanting Merrilee to stay. "The only reason Jim's been able to justify his relationship with Mrs. Parker is that neither you nor your mother has been around. He's living a fantasy with no one to burst his bubble."

"A fantasy that will kill him when he wakes up and realizes what he's done," Sally Mae added. "You must intervene, Merrilee, before this goes any further."

Merrilee's heart-shaped face contorted into a thoughtful frown. "I'll stay a week and assess the situation. Maybe my homecoming will snap Dad out of it. But I'm not committing to a book."

Sally Mae nodded in agreement. Grant could tell the old woman had lost the battle but had not conceded the war.

"Grant will take you home," she announced.

Merrilee cast him a questioning glance before turning to her grandmother. "Grant told me I could use your car."

Sally Mae nodded. "As soon as the battery's charged. Jay-Jay's backed up at the garage, but he said he'll get to it this afternoon."

"I've kept Grant from his work too long already. I can walk home, Nana. It's only two blocks."

Nothing had changed, Grant realized. Merrilee was home, but she still wanted nothing to do with him.

Sally Mae set her jaw in a determined line. "You have two pieces of luggage, and rain's in the forecast."

"I don't mind," Grant said quickly. "It's not out of my way."

"What about Gloria?" Merrilee asked with a challenge in her blue eyes. "Isn't she expecting you?"

Oh, lordy. Gloria.

He'd forgotten all about her, and there'd be hell to pay when he got home. There always was.

"I have to go by your house anyway," Grant said, accepting the inevitable. "No problem."

He hoped.

Merrilee pushed to her feet. "Then I won't keep you any longer. We can leave now."

Sally Mae stood and embraced her granddaughter. "Think about my book offer. We need you here, Merrilee. Your parents need you."

Grant bit his tongue to keep from voicing his opinion and went into the hall to retrieve her bags.

He'd needed Merrilee, too, all those years ago. Needed her like a man needs air. But his need hadn't been enough to keep her in Pleasant Valley.

Even knowing how much she loved her parents, he wondered if their plight would be enough to keep her here this time.

Chapter Three

In a daze of disbelief, Merrilee followed Grant to his truck. She couldn't shake the feeling she was moving through a bad dream. If the surrounding trees had started walking and talking, they wouldn't have surprised her as much as her father's bizarre and totally uncharacteristic betrayal.

"Are you sure Dad hasn't lost his reason?" she demanded of Grant when he climbed into the driver's seat beside her.

"He's not thinking straight, but he's not insane. He's been holding up his end of the practice without any problems."

"I never thought my father the type to suffer a midlife crisis. He's always seemed so steady. So dependable."

"He's not as young as he once was, and he's been pushed to his limit physically. That has to influence his emotions. And your mom's not been around to help him keep his balance."

"When's the last time he had a physical?"

Grant shrugged. "Not in the past couple years that I know of. We've been too busy."

"But he's not too busy for *Ginger.*" Merrilee's bitterness hit her stomach and, for an instant, she feared she might be sick in Grant's new truck. "I still can't believe it."

"Maybe you can nip this in the bud."

"I don't know. After what he's done, I don't see how Mom can ever forgive him."

"She loves him. Love solves a lot of problems."

"Causes problems, too."

Grant reached over, grasped her hand and threaded his warm, callused fingers through hers. His comforting touch called up powerful emotions Merrilee thought she'd buried for good.

Grant said, "I don't think love has anything to do with what's going on between your dad and Ginger."

Merrilee extricated her hand. She'd been thinking of how love had made her initial move from Pleasant Valley so hard. She'd felt as if she'd been torn in two, one half deliriously happy to be living her dream, the other half crying herself to sleep at night, missing home.

And especially Grant.

She'd managed to overcome her homesickness. And she'd confined Grant to a deep corner of her heart that she refused to visit. Whether she stayed in Pleasant Valley a day, a week, or longer, she'd make certain he remained locked away. She didn't want those wounds opened again. And, after all, he had Gloria now, so any residual feelings MJ had for Grant were moot.

In a matter of minutes he stopped the truck in front of her parents' home.

He opened his door and she put her hand on his arm. "Don't get out. I can manage my bags."

"You're sure?"

She nodded. This homecoming was difficult. She had to face it alone. She forced a smile. "Gloria's waiting, remember?"

His scowl puzzled her. "How could I forget?"

Maybe things at home weren't going well for Grant, either, but Merrilee had her own problems. "Thanks for the lift."

"Call me if you need me." Grant's brown eyes darkened to almost black with what appeared genuine concern. "I want to help."

"Thanks. I will." But, for the life of her, Merrilee couldn't think what help Grant might be. She couldn't even conjure how *she* could ward off the looming disaster.

With a farewell nod, Grant closed his door, pulled

away from the curb and gunned the engine in his hurry to return to Gloria.

Merrilee stood at the curb, studying the house where she'd lived until her college years and her subsequent move to New York. The century-old, two-story Victorian with its Queen Anne turret that held her second-floor bedroom hadn't changed. The white clapboards, set off by a dark green roof and shutters, sparkled in the sun. Her mother's beds of daffodils and tulips filled the borders with cheery color, and the blossoming red-bud tree was a splash of lavender against the white siding. Baskets of verdant Boston ferns nestled among the inviting wicker porch furniture.

Home.

MJ loved her life in New York, the bustle of activity and the ever-changing variety of the city, but she'd always held this image of home in her heart, like a treasure locked away in a bank vault whose existence gave her security and peace of mind.

With a start, she realized she'd thought of Grant that way, too. Even though she'd refused to marry him, she'd always known that he was here in Pleasant Valley, working with her father, his life unchanged since she'd left, as if waiting for her eventual return.

Except now, with Gloria, Grant had moved on. She tried to feel happy for him, but all she felt was a depressing sense of loss, which made absolutely no sense. She'd refused to marry Grant.

And now she couldn't picture herself ever marrying at all.

Merrilee climbed the porch steps, fumbled in the bottom of her purse for her key and opened the door. She was greeted by a blast of musty air instead of the usual delicious aromas emanating from the kitchen. Her footsteps on the hardwood floor echoed eerily in the empty house and suddenly it didn't seem like home at all.

She dropped her bags in the family room and sank into her father's leather recliner while she assessed the painful irony of her situation. What she'd loved most about home and Pleasant Valley was the fact that nothing ever changed.

And what she'd hated most was that nothing ever changed.

May you have what you wish for.

The old Chinese curse popped into her mind and she rued the day she'd ever longed for life in Pleasant Valley to be different.

She gazed around the familiar room at the shelves of her mother's favorite books, the sweater, folded across the back of a chair, that her mother kept downstairs in case of a sudden chill, the stack of old 45s her parents had danced to, the seed catalogs beside her father's chair and the row of framed photographs on the mantel, a pictorial chronicle of the Strattons' life as a family.

Her family's life had been happy, satisfying and filled with love and excitement. So how had things gone so horribly wrong?

That question shook MJ to her core.

Unable to dislodge her depression, she wandered upstairs to her parents' bedroom and opened the closet. Her father's side was empty, her mother's sparsely filled. If Merrilee couldn't mend the break between her parents, would they divorce and sell this house, the only real home she'd ever known? She tried but couldn't picture another family living here. Couldn't imagine her mom and dad not being together.

Merrilee sank onto the edge of the queen-size bed, remembering Sunday mornings as a child when she'd climbed in with her parents while they'd read the comics and laughed together.

The emptiness of the house taunted her and resolve hardened her backbone. She didn't know if Nana's book scheme would work, but Merrilee would give it a try. New York, fame and fortune would have to wait until she'd knitted her unraveled family back together.

GRANT OPENED HIS FRONT door and braced himself for Gloria's assault. The majestic young Irish wolfhound bounded into his arms with a whimper of delight, her long tongue washing his face. If he'd weighed a few pounds less or the dog a few more, Gloria would have knocked him off his feet.

With dismay, he surveyed the living room of the log cabin he'd spent his savings and spare time to renovate. Dacron fluff from shredded cushions littered the sofa, a drapery panel hung at a precarious angle and a disgusting wetness puddled on his laboriously refinished and highly polished pine floor.

He curbed his frustration and greeted Gloria with an affectionate hug. The dog couldn't help her separation anxiety. It wasn't her fault the medication he'd prescribed hadn't taken effect yet. He could only imagine the abuse the poor animal had suffered before he'd rescued her from the roadside, injured, dehydrated, starving, with her fur matted and dirty. Her fear of men had been a silent testament to prior mistreatment. He'd worked for weeks to earn her trust. Now if he could only cure her fear of abandonment, she'd make a perfect companion.

And, God willing, Grant thought, surveying his domain, he would accomplish that feat before she wrecked his house completely.

Gloria loved riding, and Grant usually took her on rounds with him, but he'd been reluctant to leave her in the truck at the airport. No telling what she'd have done to his new leather upholstery.

Not that Merrilee—or MJ, he corrected himself with a grunt of disapproval—would have minded Gloria's presence. She'd inherited her father's love of animals, one of the many interests she and Grant had had in common. While he mopped the floor with paper towels, then sprayed it with an enzyme cleaner and wiped again, he pondered how his encounter with his ex-fiancée had affected him.

When Sally Mae had called with the news about Jim and asked Grant to pick up Merrilee at the airport, Grant hadn't hesitated. He'd considered himself free of any hold Merrilee once had on him. After all, after the initial shock and heartbreak, he'd survived her desertion just fine, had gone on with his life as he'd planned, even with a Merrilee-size hole in his heart. He hadn't expected seeing her again to affect him.

Just as he hadn't expected to fall in love with her that summer seven years ago when he joined Jim's practice….

HIS FIRST NIGHT back in Pleasant Valley after his internship, Jim and Cat had invited him to dinner to celebrate their new partnership. Cat had answered the door and as Grant had stepped into the foyer, Merrilee had come down the stairs. Expecting the same tow-headed, irritating brat that had hung out with his little sister, Grant had been struck speechless by the maturity of the beautiful young woman whose growing up had caught him by surprise.

She'd worn a blue sundress, slightly paler than her eyes, that showed off her California tan, her pale blond hair and deliciously long legs. The clinging fabric had called subtle attention to the curve of her breasts and hips, a far cry from the flat-chested, skinny kid in jeans and T-shirts of his memory. Low-heeled sandals had made her feet with pearl-pink nails seem almost bare. But it was her smile that had captured his heart, a slow, teasing grin that shot warmth spiraling through him.

"Hey, Grant." Surprise was evident in her greeting. "Dad didn't tell me you're his new partner. I thought you'd taken a job in Georgia."

Grant was suddenly tongue-tied. The annoying kid he'd teased mercilessly for most of his life had turned into one of the most attractive and desirable women he'd ever encountered.

Cat had saved him from his embarrassing silence by chiming in. "He had, but your father talked him into coming home."

"He didn't have to twist my arm." Grant finally regained his ability to speak. "I always wanted to practice in Pleasant Valley, but didn't want to compete with Jim. Now we're on the same team."

"Come in here," Jim called from the living room. "The champagne's open. This calls for a toast."

Grant followed Cat and Merrilee into the elegant but cozy room, and Jim handed each a flute of the sparkling wine. He lifted his glass to Grant. "To a long and successful partnership."

"Amen to that," Cat added with enthusiasm and sipped her champagne.

But Jim was only warming up. He raised his glass again, this time to Merrilee. "To my princess, the best daughter a man could have."

"Oh, Daddy," she protested and blushed beneath her tan, but Grant could tell she was pleased.

"And finally," Jim continued, "but definitely not least, to the love of my life."

From the adoring look Jim gave Cat as he toasted her and judging by her beaming response, Grant had no doubt of the bond between the couple. As dinner progressed, they were so obviously in tune with each other, they sometimes finished one another's sentences.

After the meal, Cat shooed Grant and Merrilee out of the dining room. "Jim and I will clean up. I'm sure you two have lots of catching up to do. There's a nice breeze on the porch."

Grant checked for signs of matchmaking in Cat's expression, but his partner's wife gave no indication of guile or intrigue. Apparently, she was simply being a good hostess.

He followed Merrilee to the wicker swing on the front porch and sat beside her.

"What now?" she asked.

He blinked in astonishment at her bluntness, wondering what she was expecting.

Even in the dim twilight of the late summer evening, he could see her blush as she qualified her question. "I mean, what are your plans? Will you move back in with your parents?"

Grant shook his head. "Going home is hard after living on my own so many years. I'm looking for my own place. What about you?"

"I still have a year of college left."

"And after that, are you coming back to Pleasant Valley?"

Merrilee looked at him as if he'd grown two heads. "What would I do here?"

"Teach, like your mom. Isn't that what you'd always planned, if I recall Jodie's incessant chatter correctly?"

She smoothed her skirt with long, slender fingers, the kind a man liked to lace his own through. Her expression turned thoughtful, almost introspective. "I had planned to teach before I realized there's a world out there. I feel sometimes as if I've spent the first eighteen years of my life in isolation."

"Aw, c'mon." He felt mildly offended by her put-down of their hometown. "Pleasant Valley's a great place. You make it sound like the end of the earth."

Merrilee extended her toes to give the swing a push

and the faint rush of air caused her honeysuckle scent to swirl around him, mixing with the fragrances from Cat's perennial borders. The effect was intoxicating and he had to make an effort to concentrate on her words.

"The people here are terrific, but life's so…so *predictable*."

"And that's bad?" Her scent stirred his blood and accelerated his pulse, but somehow he managed to keep the conversation moving in spite of the distraction.

"Not if you *like* small town country living."

"And you don't?"

She shook her head. "I can't wait to leave after college. I intend to rent an apartment in New York, probably downtown, where all the artists and musicians live."

"Are you going to be a writer?"

"What makes you think that?"

"I thought you were majoring in English, like your mom."

"I'd planned to, but I switched my sophomore year to Fine Arts. I'm a photographer."

"You can take pictures in Pleasant Valley."

He couldn't understand why Merrilee, with her wonderful parents and a town filled with family and friends, would want to pack up and leave. Then he recalled how anxious he'd been to get away from Pleasant Valley his freshman year in college. He'd done a lot of traveling and, after several years away, he'd learned to appreciate home. In fact he'd reached the conclusion that Pleasant Valley was about as close to heaven as a man could get.

"I tell you what." He wanted to spare her the same learning curve. "Spend some time with me this summer and I'll show you all kinds of things to photograph."

The thought of sharing his spare time with the suddenly grown up and alluring Merrilee appealed to him on several levels.

She cocked a feathery eyebrow, her gaze skeptical. "I love animals, but—"

"I promise to vary the subject matter. And I bet I can show you at least two dozen good reasons *not* to leave Pleasant Valley."

Her skepticism didn't dim. "I'm not changing my mind."

"But you're afraid you might?"

A slow smile lifted her delectably rosy lips. "Not a bit. In fact, I'll bet I can win you over to my point of view."

"Not a chance."

"I love a challenge." Her grin widened. "When's your first day off?"

"I don't start work until next week. How about tomorrow?"

She lowered her lashes before casting him a flirtatious glance. "You don't waste any time, do you?"

He shook his head. "By the end of the summer, Merrilee June, I promise, you'll hate going back to California."

She angled her chin in defiance. "By the end of the summer, my dad will be looking for a new partner."

Alarm jolted him. "My intentions are honorable."

She giggled, a pleasant sound like a creek bubbling over stones. "I'm sure they are. I meant that when I get through with you, Grant Nathan, you'll find Pleasant Valley as boring as I do. You'll be ready to move on."

Anxious to prove her wrong, he picked her up at ten the next morning. In shorts, T-shirt and sneakers, and with her blond hair pulled back in a ponytail, she looked for an instant like the child he remembered. But closer scrutiny revealed the womanly curves beneath her casual clothes, the maturity in the attractive angles of her heart-shaped face and the intelligence in her bright blue eyes.

He opened the passenger door of the pickup for her to climb inside. His vantage point provided a clear view of her long, tanned legs, crossed demurely at the ankles, and caused heat to curl below his stomach.

"Where are we going?" she asked.

"It's a surprise." He closed the door and took a deep breath of morning air to cool his thoughts as he circled the truck and slid onto the driver's seat.

"I like surprises. That's one reason I want to move. Nothing ever surprises me in Pleasant Valley."

"I've found something that will." He started the engine, pulled away from the curb and headed downtown. He ignored her dubious expression.

After a few short blocks he turned into a diagonal parking space on Piedmont Avenue, the main drag.

"Not the hardware store," she said with obvious disappointment. "Your dad's owned this place my entire life. No surprises here."

"We're not going to the hardware store." He felt a rush of satisfaction, knowing that Merrilee would be not merely surprised, but amazed. He hadn't learned this tidbit of information himself until yesterday.

On the sidewalk he grasped her elbow and guided her toward the small storefront to the left of the hardware store. The windows were smudged with grime and a fading sign hung at an angle above the door.

"Here we are," he announced with a flourish.

Merrilee's jaw dropped. "Mr. Weatherstone's old fix-it shop? It's been empty for years."

"Hard to maintain a business repairing typewriters and small appliances in today's market," Grant agreed.

He stepped to the glass front door, so grimy it obscured the shop's interior, and gave three sharp knocks. "You should have brought your camera."

"Yeah, right." She grimaced in distaste. "So I can shoot a fascinating montage of dust motes, dead spiders and cobwebs—"

The door swung inward and an excited squeal interrupted her midsentence. "Merrilee! You're back!"

Jodie Nathan barreled through the doorway and enveloped Merrilee in a bear hug. Merrilee returned her embrace with a dazed expression.

"Jodie, what are you doing here?" Merrilee asked.

Jodie beamed at Grant and contentment flooded him. He hadn't seen his sister this happy in a long time. Her hazel eyes sparkled beneath the light brown curls that had escaped from the blue bandanna tying back her hair. Even with a smudge of dirt across one cheek, she looked radiant.

His sister tugged Merrilee inside and Grant followed.

Jodie, arms flung wide, pirouetted in the center of the floor in front of the old service counter. "Isn't it wonderful? It's all mine."

"Yours?" Merrilee shook her head, plainly bewildered. "You're going to open a fix-it shop?"

Jodie stopped her spiral and faced Merrilee, eyes shining. "You're looking at the future home of Jodie's Mountain Crafts and Café."

Merrilee looked stunned.

Grant laughed. "I said you'd be surprised."

"The building's narrow, but it's deep," Jodie explained. "There's room up front for counter service— I'll only offer breakfast and lunch. I'll cut a wide hallway down the side with shelving to display mountain crafts and supplies, and Grant's helping Dad build a deck out back for more seating. Customers can gaze across the river at the mountains while they eat."

"Wow," Merrilee said. "When did you dream this up? You never mentioned it in your letters."

"I'm tired of working for others at practically minimum wage. Living with Mom and Dad, I've saved my money, just waiting for a place downtown to come on the market. When Mrs. Weatherstone listed this yesterday, I jumped at it. Dad and Grant co-signed for the mortgage."

"See, things do change in Pleasant Valley." Grant didn't try to keep the satisfaction from his voice.

"By the time you graduate next year," Jodie said to Merrilee, "I'll have the place up and running. We can be partners. With your background in art, you can run the crafts end of the business and I'll handle the cooking and serving."

Merrilee's face crumpled. "Oh, Jodie, I hope you're not counting on me—"

"I'm doing this no matter what," his sister announced with steely determination. "If you want to be a part of it, though, we'll have a ball."

"Where's Brittany?" Merrilee abruptly changed the subject, quashing Grant's hope for a partnership between her and his sister.

"At school." Jodie's expression softened at the mention of her daughter. "I can't believe my baby's almost through first grade."

But not even her precious daughter could distract Jodie from her dream. She gave Merrilee and Grant the grand tour of every nook and cranny of the old building. Grant left with a coating of dust and mixed feelings. Jodie's work was cut out for her, but he'd never seen her so pleased or excited.

Merrilee had expressed delight over Jodie's enterprise, but she hadn't shown the slightest interest in participating, not even when Jodie had suggested she keep a running exhibit of her photographs in the shop.

Grant couldn't fault Merrilee, however. She remained Jodie's staunchest friend. When his sister had discovered she was pregnant at age fifteen and decided to keep her baby, Merrilee had stood beside Jodie, her support and loyalty never wavering, even when most of Jodie's other friends had disappeared into the woodwork.

He'd hoped the offer of a partnership with Jodie would change Merrilee's mind about not returning to Pleasant Valley, but he wasn't ready to admit defeat. After all, he had the entire summer ahead to plead his case.

THE WET SWIPE of Gloria's tongue across his face brought Grant roughly back to the present. A lot had changed in seven years. Jodie's café and craft shop were thriving. Grant had his own home. His niece, Brittany, had grown into a teenage terror. And his usually down-to-earth partner was suffering a midlife crisis that threatened to ruin a story-book marriage.

What hadn't altered was Merrilee's refusal to remain in Pleasant Valley a minute longer than necessary. And, Grant realized with a start, neither had his own stubborn determination to change her mind.

Chapter Four

In her turret bedroom, MJ laid her head on Grant's broad, tanned chest and entwined her bare arms and legs with his. He stroked her hair with a gentle hand and pressed his lips against her forehead.

"Everything's going to be all right, Merrilee." His deep voice rumbled through the muscles beneath her cheek. "You'll see."

She snuggled closer, taking comfort in his words and soaking up his body heat. "Are you talking about us or my parents?"

When he didn't answer, her eyes flew open.

SHE FOUND HERSELF ALONE, her pillow clutched in her arms. She hadn't dreamed about Grant in months and the experience left her dissatisfied, lonely and uneasy about the future.

The extraordinary quiet must have awakened her so early. Only the trill of a mockingbird in the sugar maple outside her window broke the silence now. She missed the constant growl of New York voices and the screech and grind of traffic on the street below her apartment, a cacophony she'd grown accustomed to over the years.

Staring at the ceiling, she analyzed why home didn't feel like home. The house's eerie quiet lacked its usual peacefulness and sense of refuge. Her thoughts swirled and her heart ached as she pushed aside remnants of the too real dream of Grant to contemplate the breach between her parents.

Yesterday afternoon, after Jay-Jay had recharged the battery on Nana's car, MJ had driven her grandmother to Asheville. They'd lost their way twice before locating the forlorn complex of inexpensive student housing, badly in need of a gardener, new roofs and a coat of paint. MJ had shuddered, unable to imagine her mother with her fastidious taste and love of order and pretty things living in such a place. Both her parents had morphed into strangers in the months since she'd seen them last.

The dereliction of the off-campus property had been nothing compared to her mother's distress. One look at Cat's pale, stricken face when she opened the door informed MJ that her mother already knew the horrible news.

"Your father called this morning," Cat explained after embracing her in a welcoming hug.

Anger surged through MJ; if her father had been in the room, she'd have smacked him. So totally unlike the man she'd loved and respected all her life, he hadn't had the nerve or decency to tell her mother face-to-face about his terrible betrayal.

Maybe Nana and Grant were wrong and her dad really had gone bonkers.

"His callousness is consistent with his erratic behavior." Nana's tone was biting as she cleared a stack of books and papers from the faded sofa before taking a seat. "If Jim Stratton was in his right mind, he wouldn't act so cowardly."

Cat sank into a chair as if her body could no longer support itself. When she spoke, her voice was as limp as her muscles. "It's not all Jim's fault."

Nana gazed at her sharply. "Don't tell me *you've* been dallying, too."

MJ caught her breath at her grandmother's accusation and waited for her mother's answer while the unfolding scenario grew more and more unreal.

"Don't be silly, Mother," Cat said with a weak smile. "I'm too busy working on my dissertation to have time for extracurricular activities." Her expression crumpled, her usually cheerful countenance seemingly on the verge of tears. "That's the problem. If I'd been home, looking after Jim as I'm supposed to, things would never have progressed this far."

"Fiddlesticks," Nana said heatedly. "Nothing excuses his behavior. He should know better."

Cat shook her head. "He wasn't himself when he spoke to me. He sounded strangely detached."

"You need to come home, Mom," MJ insisted. "Between the two of us—"

"I can't come home," Cat said with an uncharacteristic flatness to her usually bubbly voice. For a woman who'd often been mistaken for MJ's sister, she appeared to have aged decades since MJ last saw her.

Nana bristled. "If your Ph.D. is more important than your husband—"

"That's not it, Mother," Cat said sadly. "I know Jim. If I confront him, his stubborn streak will kick in. The more we try to sway him from this Ginger Parker slut, the more determined he'll be to prove he's doing the right thing."

MJ felt as if she were living in a bad dream. She had never considered her father the stubborn type, but then, she'd never thought of him as a philanderer, either.

"Mom, you can't just stay here and do nothing," she protested.

"I'll be better off here," Cat said with obvious unhappiness. "It's as clear as the nose on your face that your father has blocked me and our marriage from his mind or he wouldn't be acting this way."

"You're not going to fight?" MJ gazed at her mother with disbelief.

"Ginger Parker is clearly a woman with no morals or conscience," Nana announced with distaste. "When you fight a skunk, even if you win, you come out stinking."

Cat nodded. "I'll have to wait for Jim to come to his senses. In the meantime, at least here I won't have to face gossip and pitying looks."

"What if he doesn't come to his senses?" MJ said.

Panic filled her. Her parents' perfect marriage had been like the Holy Grail, a standard she had aspired to if she ever married, a shining beacon of the best things in life. Recognizing the imperfections in a relationship she'd always considered ideal rocked her world like a 7.0 earthquake on the Richter scale.

"Don't worry," Nana assured them both. "This insanity is only temporary."

"How can you be sure?" Cat looked hopeful for the first time.

"Jim Stratton's a good man at heart," Nana said. "His values are solid and run deep. When he slows down long enough to recognize his folly, he'll come running back to you, begging your forgiveness."

Cat frowned. "If I let him."

"Mom!" MJ gasped with surprise.

Cat reached over and squeezed MJ's hand. "Don't worry, sweetie. I haven't invested three decades of my life in this marriage to allow a cheap piece of New Jersey trash to ruin everything."

"That's the spirit." Nana rubbed her hands together with satisfaction. "I knew there was some fight left in you. Now, let me tell you what Merrilee and I have planned."

Her mother had listened to Nana's proposal about the photographic essay and her spirits appeared to lift slightly, but when the trio had gone out to supper at a fast-food restaurant afterward, Cat had only played with her food. After a promise by MJ to visit Cat often at her apartment, they'd said goodbye.

Upon returning to her parents' dark and empty home, MJ had been so depressed, she'd gone immediately to bed. If she hadn't been exhausted from staying up the previous night, her worries would have kept her awake, but she'd dropped off instantly.

And dreamed of Grant.

She flung the covers back and strode toward the shower. Not only did she need to reconcile her parents quickly for their sakes, she had to get out of Pleasant Valley before Grant worked his magic on her again.

Gloria, she reminded herself. As long as Grant had a new love, he'd leave MJ alone.

Another reason to leave quickly, she decided. She didn't want to hang around a minute longer than necessary to observe Grant's newfound happiness.

AFTER BREAKFAST MJ drove through town and headed west. The peaceful, sheltered valley for which the town was named unfolded before her. Deep, lush grass filled the rolling pastures along the narrow, winding road that followed the meandering course of the Piedmont River, swollen with melted snow and frothing white as it rushed over its rock-filled bed. Mountains rose on either side of the valley, their slopes colored with the warm russets, silvery grays and earthy browns of trunks and branches thick with buds. Leaves would be bursting forth any day.

Her camera sat ready on the seat beside her and, although she passed several scenes that provided fantastic shots, MJ didn't stop. She'd only be postponing the inevitable and she wanted to get through this initial awkward meeting with her father as soon as possible.

Conflicting emotions warred inside her. Anger for the pain he was causing her mother battled with pity for his emotional state that allowed such uncharacteristic behavior. MJ prayed she'd find the right approach. If she alienated her father, Nana's scheme wouldn't stand a chance of success.

The thought of having a stepmother named Ginger strengthened MJ's resolve. And scared the living daylight out of her. She hoped she wouldn't have to meet the woman. She didn't trust herself to keep her anger and disgust under control.

Around the next river bend, MJ caught sight of the clinic, a long, low building of rustic clapboards with a green-metal roof. Behind were dog runs enclosed by chain-link fences and a matching barn and corral that included a quarantine area for large farm animals. Her father's car wasn't in the parking lot when she pulled in, but he often parked behind the barn, out of sight.

With a queasiness in her stomach, MJ left the car, climbed the front steps and entered the waiting room. Its only occupant was a middle-aged woman with a butterball of a Yorkshire terrier on her lap. There was also a young Irish wolfhound curled at her feet.

MJ crossed to the reception desk, separated by a sliding window from the waiting room, and rapped on the glass.

Fran Dillard slid the window open. "Merrilee June! What are you doing home?"

The elderly receptionist, who'd been with the clinic since its beginning, had no sooner spoken than she stammered in confusion to cover her gaff.

"I mean, it's, uh, good to see you. It's been over a year, hasn't it?"

An intelligent woman who'd helped keep the business end of the practice running smoothly for three decades, Fran apparently had guessed why MJ had returned to Pleasant Valley.

MJ answered quickly to ease the receptionist's discomfort. "It's good to see you, too, Fran. Is Daddy with a client?"

Fran shook her head, then tucked an errant gray strand from her French twist behind her ear. Her brown eyes shimmered with unspoken sympathy but her tone was business-like. "He's out of the office all day."

"Oh." MJ didn't ask where, afraid Fran might say Ginger Parker's.

"Is that you, Merrilee?" Grant's voice sounded from one of the examining rooms.

She cursed silently at the corresponding flip-flop of her heart and took a deep breath before answering, hoping to sound nonchalant. "I came to see Daddy."

"I have one more client." Grant popped his head around a door, looking, if anything, even more attractive than he had yesterday in a beige British walking sweater with brown suede patches on the shoulders and elbows that matched the hue of his eyes. "Can you wait?"

"Sure."

With her meeting with her father postponed, she had nothing else to do. And asking Grant her father's whereabouts would be less embarrassing than asking Fran. Somehow not acknowledging her dad's indiscretion to others made his treachery seem less real, even though she knew her attitude was irrational.

She settled into a chair in the waiting room and picked up an issue of *Dog* magazine. She was leafing through, admiring the artistry of the photographs, when she felt a pressure on her knee. The Irish wolfhound had left its owner and placed its head in MJ's lap. The middle-aged woman didn't appear to notice, so MJ petted the dog's large regal head. Its soulful eyes locked on hers and she felt an instant kinship with the animal, as if it were telling her it understood her distress.

"Dr. Nathan will see you now, Mrs. Ware," Fran announced.

The middle-aged woman with the Yorkie under her arm stepped through the door to the examining rooms and the wolfhound followed.

GRANT DISPATCHED Mrs. Ware and Bon-bon with strict orders to limit the canine's food intake. The dog was aptly named. Its owner was constantly plying it with treats, which resulted in its creeping obesity.

According to Fran, his ten-thirty appointment was a no-show, so he was glad to have time for Merrilee. Thoughts of her had kept him awake last night. He'd been plagued for years by nagging questions she'd never answered about breaking their engagement, and he welcomed an opportunity to demand some answers and to get a few things off his chest.

He strode to the waiting room door. "Come on in, Merrilee. I'm free for a few minutes before my next appointment."

Merrilee tossed aside the magazine she'd been reading and followed him down the narrow hall to his office.

Grant took satisfaction in the impeccable neatness

of the small room with its bay window overlooking the barn. A handful of file folders lay on the desk beside the computer monitor, the only items not in their proper place. In uncharacteristic self-analysis, he wondered if he cultivated order in his office to make up for the shambles he'd made of his love life.

Merrilee sat in the leather club chair he offered and he settled in the one behind his desk. She wore her pale blond hair in an alluring French braid. Dressed in designer jeans, calf-hugging boots that looked like Italian leather, and a navy cable-knit sweater that accented the blue of her eyes, she retained the wholesome good looks of a homecoming queen. Her years in New York, however, had added a polish of sleek sophistication, creating a knock-out effect.

She surveyed his office with a quick glance. "I'd forgotten how organized you are."

"You make it sound like a vice."

She shrugged. "Not unless you're compulsive about it."

"I like to think of myself as amazingly efficient." He noted the smudges of fatigue beneath her eyes and the tired slump of her shoulders. Damn. Now definitely wasn't the time for confrontation. His questions would have to wait. "You okay?"

Merrilee appeared to fight back tears. "Seeing Mom last night was tough."

"How's she holding up?"

"Not well. She put up a brave front for Nana and me, but I can tell she's devastated. Where's Daddy?"

"Thompson's dairy. He's vaccinating the herd. It's an all-day job."

"So he's not avoiding me?"

"He's not aware you're in town, as far as I know. You sure you're okay? You look pale."

"I'd psyched myself up for seeing him, hoping to spend the day with him. Now I'll have to wait till tomorrow."

"Merrilee—" He paused, uncertain how to continue.

"Yes?" She lifted her gaze and he felt himself drowning in her sad blue eyes.

"Forget it. Your family dilemma isn't any of my business." After all, Grant was no longer family.

She cocked her head in an appealing little-girl fashion he remembered so vividly. "Nana dragged you smack into the middle of this, whether you want to be or not. That gives you the right to speak your mind."

He took a deep breath and dived in head-first. "I'm worried about you."

"Me? Daddy's the one with the problem."

Grant shook his head. "You know how you are, Merrilee June."

"MJ."

"Whatever," he said with exasperation.

She arched an eyebrow. "How am I?"

"You're a patron saint of lost causes."

She bristled before his eyes. "What's that supposed to mean."

"Admit it," he said gently. "You're always off on some crusade. As early as middle school, you were recruiting Jodie to help you protect the rain forests or save the whales."

Her eyes flashed blue fire. "And we did some good. Don't forget, we kept the city from tearing down the old railroad depot. It's the historical society museum now, thanks to our efforts."

He nodded to concede her point. "But your campaign to ban fur coats turned out differently." He couldn't contain his grin.

She scowled. "What's so funny?"

"The only woman in Pleasant Valley who owned a fur coat was your nana."

"She still owns it," Merrilee admitted with a rueful smile.

"That's what's so funny." Grant's grin faded. "But this scheme you and your grandmother have hatched is much more personal than your other crusades. I don't want you hurt if it fails."

Merrilee's back stiffened and her chin jutted at a defiant angle. "It has to work."

Grant fought the urge to round the desk and pull her into his arms. She was determined to save Jim from the clutches of the "other woman," but Grant wasn't sure his partner wanted saving. If Jim had been thinking clearly, he wouldn't be in Ginger Parker's clutches in the first place.

"You have to accept the possibility that your nana's plan won't work," he said with a tenderness he hoped took the sting from his words. "And, if it doesn't, you must realize that the failure won't be your fault. Your father's a grown man. I think what he's doing is a mistake, but I also know he has the right to make one, if he chooses."

"You're wrong," she said hotly, indignation staining her high cheekbones a deep rose. "He has no right, not when what he chooses breaks my mother's heart and betrays his marriage vows."

Merrilee had offered the perfect opening to remind her of her promise to marry Grant and how she'd broken his heart, but he bit back the bitter words. He'd have to be a sadist to say anything now that would add to her distress.

Besides, their relationship was water under the bridge.

Then why did his heart ache at the sight of her? And why was he so concerned about her unhappiness?

Because he still loved her.

Always would.

Not many animals mated for life. The swan was one. With an inward sigh, he admitted that Grant Nathan was another. But if he couldn't have Merrilee, at least maybe he could save her from more heartache.

"Like I said, your being here and spending time with your dad might end his affair and mend your parents' marriage, but it might not. And if it doesn't, I don't want you feeling it's your fault. Jim Stratton's made his bed. Literally."

Merrilee flinched. "I wish you hadn't painted that picture."

"It may be one you'll have to live with."

"Is this your way of saying you won't help?"

She sounded so forlorn, Grant had to squash again the desire to hold her. Instead he laced his fingers on top of his desk blotter. "I'll help you schedule time with Jim on his rounds. But if your father catches wind that you, your grandmother or I am plotting against him, the entire scheme could backfire and plant him even more firmly in Ginger Parker's clutches."

"You're right." She seemed to force a smile. "You should have been a therapist. Your counseling talents are wasted on animals."

"But they come in handy with their owners."

He wished he could help Merrilee more with her father's problem. She seemed so fragile and vulnerable, nothing like the headstrong and fiercely independent woman who'd struck out on her own to conquer New York and the world.

"What are your plans for today?" he asked.

"Nana has her Rook club and Mom has classes. I'll stay busy preparing proofs of pictures from my latest job." She frowned. "I can't believe it was only night before last that I photographed that wedding."

Grant guessed that the prospect of viewing photos of a deliriously happy bride and groom was depressing under the circumstances. She needed a friend, someone she could talk to about her parents' breakup. And she also needed to get her mind off their problems for a while.

"I have appointments until two-thirty this afternoon," Grant said. "After that, I promised Jeff Davidson I'd drive up to check his livestock. Want to come?"

"Jeff Davidson?" The name seemed to shock Merrilee momentarily out of her depression. "I thought Pleasant Valley's resident bad boy had joined the army."

"Marines. But he didn't re-up after his last tour of duty and now he's home to stay. Come with me when I call on him. It'll take your mind off…things. You shouldn't be alone. Too much time to think."

Merrilee took only a few seconds to contemplate his offer and answered with obvious relief. "I'd like that. Thanks."

Grant nodded, pleased she'd agreed. Against his better judgment he added, "And come to my house for supper afterward."

"Shouldn't you check with Gloria first?"

At the irony in her tone, he couldn't tell whether she knew Gloria was a dog and was teasing, or if she really hadn't a clue that there'd never be another woman in his life. At least no one serious.

"Gloria loves company." He'd introduce the wolf-hound to Merrilee this afternoon. Although gun-shy around most men, Gloria adored women.

Merrilee shoved to her feet with apparent reluctance. She probably wasn't looking forward to the hours that stretched ahead, filled with worry and unhappy thoughts. "I'll meet you here around two-thirty, then."

Grant rose, slung his arm around her shoulder with an easy familiarity in order not to spook her, and walked her out to the waiting room.

"In the meantime," he suggested, "why don't you visit Jodie? She'll be disappointed if she learns you're in town and haven't stopped by."

"I don't know…"

Grant tipped her chin with his finger and found himself gazing directly into the depths of her eyes. He wished he could erase the pain there. He suspected she was dreading encountering folks in town who had already heard the gossip about her father.

"This is the slow season for tourists at the café," he explained. "And the locals eat early. If you go after one, you'll have the place practically to yourself."

"I'll think about it," she said, "but either way, I'll meet you here later. I can take some preliminary shots when we visit Jeff, so I can honestly tell Daddy I've already started my book."

Grant gave her shoulders a squeeze and released her with reluctance. "See you later."

ON THE DRIVE BACK to town, MJ debated whether she should have accepted Grant's invitation. She admitted the possibility of opening old wounds, but she also longed to prove her heart had healed for good, and that, when the goodbyes came, this time she could walk away from Grant without regrets.

She also really, really didn't want to be alone now. She'd welcome an afternoon with the devil himself if he would take her mind off her parents' problems.

No, that wasn't true. More than anything, she wished to avoid people who might ask embarrassing questions about her folks, or even worse, a run-in with those jealous souls who would take great delight in the failure of a perfect marriage. Heaven knew, Pleasant Valley had a bumper crop of those kinds of gossips. MJ had watched them in action when Jodie was in trouble, and the prospect of those small-minded hypocrites dissecting her parents' marriage and salivating over her father's bizarre affair made her sick to her stomach.

She'd rather take her chances with Grant.

Try as she might, however, she couldn't shake the feeling of déjà vu. The prospect of going on rounds with Grant brought back recollections of the summer he'd joined her father's practice. With outrageous self-confidence, he'd bet that he could make her want to stay in Pleasant Valley forever.

And he'd won.

Temporarily.

Memories flooded back in a torrent. With Grant, she'd visited almost every farm in Pleasant Valley, places she'd called on with her father from the time she was a toddler. With Grant, however, she'd viewed old places with a fresh perspective. En route, he'd pointed out landmarks that she'd seen, but never really noticed: beds of trillium almost obscured on the shady forest floor, a hidden waterfall on Cradle Creek and a vantage point that revealed sunlight glinting off the granite rock face of Devil's Mountain like dancing flames at sunset.

Most of all, she'd observed Grant in action. In his element. Even though he'd grown up in town as the son of a merchant, he'd displayed an easy camaraderie with the farmers and their families and a tacit understanding of the hardscrabble facts of making a living off the land.

And his touch with animals had been magical.

Catching sight of the silos of the Mauney farm, set back from the road behind a small hill, MJ remembered her first visit there with Grant. Joe Mauney had found one of his cows tangled in barbed wire, its udder torn and bleeding. He hadn't been able to extricate the panicked animal because the cow wouldn't let him near it.

Grant had taken the call on his cell phone one Saturday afternoon while he and MJ were helping Jodie clean her newly acquired building before starting renovations. Driving to the farm, he'd pushed his pickup to the limits on the winding curves, sending MJ's heart into her throat more than once, but he'd maintained perfect control of the vehicle, even in his urgency.

When they'd reached the farm, Joe had met them in the barnyard and indicated the north pasture. "Hired me a new helper. He was mending fences yesterday, and the idjit left a coil of wire in the field." Joe's ancient, weathered face was grim. "Can't get the cow unhooked and she's tore up bad. You may have to put her down."

"Only as a last resort," Grant replied.

They marched into the pasture. The cow's mournful bellows could be heard long before they spotted her.

"I don't want you losing income from a good milker," Grant added.

But MJ had known Grant's concern was more for the animal than for Joe Mauney's earnings. Grant had already told her that the only part of his job he hated was having to destroy an animal he couldn't heal.

As they approached the cow, MJ saw immediately that, in its panic, the Holstein had become more snarled in the wire, causing itself more harm. The nearer they drew, the more agitated the cow became.

"Stay here," Grant said to MJ and Joe. "And keep still. I'll try to calm her."

Assessing the cow's distraught state, MJ doubted that reassuring the injured beast was possible. Undeterred, Grant took a syringe from his bag, filled it with tranquilizer and walked slowly toward the animal.

"Easy, there." He spoke softly, soothingly. "It's going to be all right. I'm here to help."

MJ knew the cow wasn't intelligent enough to understand his words. She held her breath. If the huge bovine decided to lash out with its hooves, it could cause Grant serious injury, even kill him. Grant also ran the risk of entangling himself in the treacherous wire.

Amazingly, the longer Grant spoke in his low, gentle voice, the quieter the animal grew. Grant came within reach, and ran his hand slowly over the cow's head and down its withers. His touch seemed to soothe the animal's fear. Even before Grant jabbed it with the tranquilizer, the cow ceased bellowing and thrashing.

"Damnedest thing I ever saw," Joe muttered under his breath. "Like he cast a spell on it."

"Tranquilizers are amazing," MJ said.

Joe shook his head. "Doc had that cow steady before giving it a shot. Must have magic hands."

Once the drug had taken effect, Joe held the animal's head while Grant used wire cutters to free the beast. Then he stitched the long, jagged tears on the udder.

After Grant had given Joe antibiotics and instructions for the Holstein's care, they'd left the farm with the farmer's gratitude ringing in their ears.

MJ recalled the incident as if it had happened yesterday. As she approached the downtown district, she tried but failed to quell other haunting memories of the touch of Grant's magic hands.

Chapter Five

Grant had been right about the tourist season. As MJ drove into town, she couldn't spot a single car with an out-of-state tag. Visitors would wait for summer and warmer weather before trekking through town to the mountains. Today, even local traffic was light and she found a parking space directly in front of Jodie's Mountain Crafts and Café.

Her friend's renovations had been ongoing over the past seven years, replacing all vestiges of the derelict Weatherstone fix-it shop. Log siding gave the building the rustic look of an old mountain lodge, and the huge sparkling display windows and double-glass doors projected a sense of openness and welcome. The jaunty awning of burgundy and hunter-green stripes above the door was new, another sign of Jodie's success.

MJ stepped inside and almost turned and fled. She should have taken Grant's advice to wait until after the lunch hour, because the counter was crowded with men and women who worked downtown. Fortunately, they were all either concentrating on their food or engrossed in conversation, and no one noticed her.

Visible in the open kitchen, Maria, the new short-order cook Jodie had mentioned in her last e-mail, worked the grill. Jodie stood at the cash register just inside the door, making change for a departing customer.

When she caught sight of MJ, her face registered surprise, then pleasure. "I'll be right with you."

MJ couldn't run now, so she studied the day's special on the chalkboard set on an easel. With her mind in turmoil, nothing she read registered.

Jodie appeared at her elbow. "The Virginia stew's good. Mom's family recipe."

"I'm not really hungry. I just came to talk, but—" She nodded at the busy counter.

"Everyone's been served. Things should quiet down soon." Her old friend smiled with a mixture of pleasure and compassion. "You can eat on the deck. It's more private."

"And freezing." MJ shuddered at the thought of the cold wind blowing off the river.

Jodie shook her head. "Not anymore. I have something new. It isn't finished yet, but if you don't mind roughing it… Brynn's having lunch there. You can sit with her."

"Thanks." MJ gave Jodie a hug. "It's good to see you. And great to see the café doing so well."

Jodie returned her embrace, then led her through the

wide hallway lined with shelves of craft supplies and merchandise, everything from handmade pottery and quilts to rustic birdhouses. Sunshine streamed through huge skylights to illuminate the items, and MJ's artist's eye appreciated their creative arrangement and immaculate condition. In spite of the size and intricacy of her inventory, Jodie never let a speck of dust linger in her shop. And, unless Jodie had changed, the café kitchen was equally spotless.

"I figured you'd show up soon," Jodie said once they were out of earshot of the lunch crowd.

MJ stopped and faced her. "Oh, lordy, Jodie. Does everyone in town know?"

"You know Pleasant Valley," Jodie said with an unhappy frown. "Gossip travels like wildfire through a dry thicket."

MJ felt a rush of compassion for Jodie, who'd endured the brunt of community gossip and censure fourteen years ago when Brittany had arrived out of wedlock. Jodie had not only survived but thrived. That fact gave MJ a glimmer of hope that her parents might somehow weather their current storm.

At the back of the shop Jodie stepped onto what had once been an open deck, and MJ followed. She glanced around in surprise. "You didn't tell me."

Jodie flashed a satisfied smile. "Wanted to wait until I'd finished decorating, and I'm almost through. What do you think?"

Panels of insulated glass arched over the deck, forming a huge conservatory that provided a clear view of both the river and the mountain ridges that ringed the valley. Dining tables had been carefully arranged between groupings of potted palms and ficus to provide an oasis of privacy for each party. Despite the chilly temperature outside, the room was comfortably warm.

A woman rose from a seat at a corner table, and if MJ hadn't been expecting Brynn, she wouldn't have immediately recognized her longtime friend. Brynn's bright red hair had darkened to an attractive auburn and grown from short curls into a sleek, shoulder-length cut. She was out of uniform in snug jeans, a fisherman's sweater and tooled leather boots, an outfit that showcased a body that made men's mouths water. Her midnight-blue eyes danced with delight as she approached and gave MJ a warm hug.

"It's great to see you, Merrilee."

"Good to see you, too, Brynn."

"I'll bring you lunch," Jodie offered MJ. "What do you want?"

"You choose," MJ said. "I'm not really hungry."

"Bless your heart. Comfort food it is, then," Jodie said and returned to the kitchen.

"Sit with me." Brynn guided MJ toward the table she'd vacated. "I'm sorry I couldn't say more when you called the other night. Didn't think it was my business."

MJ sank into a chair across from Brynn. "Nana's filled me in on all the sordid details."

Brynn's mouth twisted with contempt. "I knew that Yankee was trouble the minute she hit town."

MJ couldn't help grinning. "Some things never change. For an otherwise open-minded person, you're still blindly biased when it comes to Northerners."

"Don't know how you stand living in the midst of them, although I admit I have met a few Yankees I've liked." Brynn added artificial sweetener and stirred her coffee. "It's the ones who treat me as if I'm mentally deficient that get my dander up. The ones who think Southerners are stupid because they speak with a drawl. Pshaw!"

MJ let her friend rant. For all her Yankee-bashing, Brynn was no bigot. If anyone needed Officer Sawyer's assistance, whether with directions, car trouble or any other emergency, regional differences flew out the window and Brynn was standing tall, ready and eager to help, no matter who needed it.

"I ran a background check on this Ginger Parker," Brynn said.

"Because she's from New Jersey?" Surprise jolted MJ. Maybe Brynn's prejudice against Yankees ran deeper than MJ had realized.

Brynn sipped her coffee, then shook her head. "Because she was throwing herself at my uncle Bud. Aunt Marion was ready to commit murder, so as an officer of the law, I felt it my duty to do a little snooping."

Brynn's uncle, Bud Sawyer, ran the local real estate company and was also president of the chamber of commerce. He and Marion had been married even longer than MJ's parents. No wonder Brynn didn't like Ginger Parker, Yankee or not.

"Find anything interesting?" MJ asked.

Brynn nodded. "When the infamous Mrs. Parker came to town, first thing she did was join the Baptist church. Played the grieving widow and virtuous woman to the hilt. Had all the men and half the women in Pleasant Valley feeling sorry for her recent bereavement."

"Played the widow? You mean, she isn't one?"

"Oh, she's a widow, all right. But her husband died eleven years ago."

"But—"

Brynn held up her hand. "I know what you're thinking. Some women grieve for the rest of their lives. But this skank is a fake from the get-go. Turns out she hated her husband. I checked with the police department of the New Jersey town where they lived. For a decade before he died, the police logged over two dozen complaints of domestic disturbances. Those two fought like heavyweight contenders."

MJ shivered. What kind of person had her father hooked up with?

"And that's not all," Brynn added. "Just before Mrs. Parker moved south, she changed her name. Her husband wasn't a Parker."

"That's strange," MJ said. "I mean, if she hated him, why wait so long after he died to ditch his name?"

"I'm still checking," Brynn said.

Anger boiled in MJ at the woman who'd thrown so many lives into chaos. "Wish I could think of a way to run her out of town."

"If you come up with a plan that doesn't break any laws, I'll be happy to help. Thank God, Uncle Bud got her number. Wish your dad was as lucky."

Jodie, carrying a food-laden tray, crossed the deck. She set the tray on a nearby rack and placed several dishes in front of MJ and Brynn.

"Virginia stew and homemade biscuits for you, Merrilee. And dessert for Brynn."

"I didn't order dessert," Brynn said forcefully but gazed at the dish with unmistakable longing. "I have to fit into my uniforms."

"It's blackberry cobbler à la mode, but I can take it back," Jodie offered.

"Touch that bowl and I'll have to shoot you." Brynn succumbed with a grin and took a bite. "Where'd you get blackberries this time of year?"

"I pick all summer and keep a freezer full." Jodie placed a coffeepot and mug in front of a third chair, poured herself a cup and joined them. "Have you seen Grant?" she asked MJ.

"He picked me up at the airport." MJ kept her tone

casual, knowing Jodie was digging for more. Her friend never tired of her campaign to enlist MJ as her sister-in-law.

At MJ's announcement, Brynn shook her fingers as if she'd touched something hot. "Caroline Tuttle won't be happy about that."

MJ raised her eyebrows. Grant had dated Caroline in high school. "She's still in town?"

"And still single," Brynn said.

"And more determined than ever to become Mrs. Grant Nathan." Jodie added French vanilla cream to her mug of steaming coffee.

"She needn't worry about me," MJ said. "She should worry about Gloria."

Jodie and Brynn exchanged amused looks over their coffee mugs.

"Gloria?" they asked in unison.

"I know she's living with Grant." MJ sensed she had missed something. "What's so funny?"

"Guess you haven't met Gloria." Brynn looked as if she was trying not to laugh. "She's a real dog."

MJ shrugged. "Well, if Grant thinks she's pretty—"

Jodie and Brynn burst into laughter and MJ realized instantly that she'd been so worried over her parents that she'd missed the obvious.

"Gloria *is* a dog," she said with chagrin at her own stupidity.

"An Irish wolfhound," Brynn said. "I found her by the side of the highway up near Devil's Mountain. She'd been hit by a car, so I called Grant."

"Grant worked a miracle with that poor animal," Jodie said with more than a hint of pride. "She'd been badly abused before the hit-and-run. She was underfed, mangy and terrified of men. Now she thinks the sun rises and sets with Grant."

MJ remembered the wolfhound in the waiting room. "I've seen that dog, but I didn't know she belonged to Grant."

"They're inseparable," Jodie said. "She goes everywhere with him."

Oh boy, MJ thought with a sinking sensation in her stomach. Gloria wasn't Grant's new love interest, so when MJ had supper with him tonight, they'd be alone. But no problem, she assured herself. The turmoil she felt when she was with Grant was merely echoes of spent emotions, like the twinges an amputee experiences from ghost nerve endings in a limb long gone. She could handle being alone with him.

She hoped.

"You all right, Merrilee?"

MJ looked up to find Jodie studying her with a commiserating look.

"I don't know," she answered honestly.

She pushed aside bothersome thoughts of Grant and told them Nana's plan for her pictorial essay.

"Haven't got a clue whether my being around Daddy will do any good," she admitted when she'd finished.

"If there's anything we can do," Jodie said, "just ask."

Brynn nodded. "Me, too."

MJ strove to lighten the moment before her friends's empathy made her cry. "Don't suppose Jodie could poison Ginger's coffee the next time she comes in?"

Jodie scowled fiercely, contorting her usually complacent features. "If I thought I could get away with it…"

Brynn brightened. "Maybe you could sue the woman."

"For what?" MJ asked.

"You know lawyers," Brynn said with an expression of distaste. "They don't need a reason, just a retainer."

MJ suppressed a smile. Brynn had less use for attorneys than she had for Yankees.

Brynn looked thoughtful. "On the basis of her tacky wardrobe, I could arrest her for indecent exposure."

Bolstered by her friends's loyalty and affection, MJ laughed. "You two haven't changed."

The years fell away, and they could have been teenagers again, huddled over cherry-flavored Cokes in the back booth of Paulie's Drug Store and swooning at the new math teacher's uncanny resemblance to Harrison Ford. MJ had made friends in New York, but none who knew and understood her as these two did.

Brynn finished the last bite of her cobbler and looked at her watch. "Gotta go. Have some errands to run before my shift starts."

"What time is it?" MJ asked.

When Brynn told her, MJ shoved aside her untouched food. "Better bring me the check, Jodie."

Jodie shook her head. "Lunch is on me. You meeting your father?"

"Not today. I'm making rounds with Grant this afternoon."

Brynn and Jodie exchanged glances and Jodie grinned. "Just like the old days."

"Don't go matchmaking, Jodie Nathan," MJ warned her. "As soon as I get my father's head straight, I'm heading back to New York."

Brynn shook her head.

"What?" MJ insisted.

"Grant hasn't so much as looked at another woman since you broke your engagement," Brynn said. "He's still in love with you, Merrilee."

MJ tamped down the old feelings Brynn's words conjured. She opted for anger instead. "And I'm supposed to marry a man just because he loves me."

Brynn wasn't easily deterred. "Sounds like a good start."

"I notice neither of you has a husband," MJ said pointedly. "Why the push to get me hitched?"

"When would I find time for a husband?" Brynn asked.

"And after what I've been through, I'm off men for life. But Grant would be good for you," Jodie insisted with sisterly loyalty.

"Ah…" MJ softened her expression, unable to maintain the pretension of anger. "But would I be good for Grant?"

GRANT CHECKED THE TIME. Twenty past three and no sign of Merrilee. She'd stood him up without even calling to say she wasn't coming.

Annoyed, he whistled for Gloria, told Fran he was leaving and headed for his truck, parked in front of the clinic. He'd hoped accompanying him this afternoon would take Merrilee's mind off her troubles, but she must have found some other diversion. His annoyance switched to concern.

Maybe she'd had an accident on a treacherous curve of the winding valley road.

He pushed that possibility away and in its place tumbled a bitter memory from six years ago when Merrilee had broken their engagement, returned his ring and shattered his world.

THE MAGNITUDE of his feelings for her had taken him by surprise that summer he'd first joined the practice, when he'd spent all his spare time with her after his off-the-cuff bet that he'd make her want to stay in Pleasant Valley. He'd given few passing thoughts to marriage before then, had figured only that someday he'd find a woman who'd be a good wife and, if he was lucky, a good friend. He hadn't expected to experience such gut-wrenching, soul-shaking passion, and had never expected it to last. But that fall, once Merrilee had returned to school, he'd suffered a loneliness unlike any he'd ever known.

That's when he'd gone shopping for a ring. He'd selected an aquamarine the color of her eyes and circled with diamonds. And when he'd slipped it on her finger the following Christmas Eve, in an attempt to show her the depth of his feelings, he'd made a complete and total fool of himself.

"Since I couldn't give you the sky and the stars, I chose this," he'd said.

Luckily, she hadn't laughed. Instead, tears of joy had sparkled in those remarkable blue eyes when she'd accepted his proposal. Although he hadn't thought it possible, at that moment she was more beautiful, funnier, more lovable than he'd remembered from their summer together.

After their engagement, however, the trouble had started almost immediately. After weeks of disagreement, they'd finally settled on a December wedding the following year in the Pleasant Valley Community

Church and a honeymoon on Florida's Longboat Key. Their sticking point had been where they would live afterward.

Although Merrilee had tentatively agreed, after Grant's all-out campaign the summer before, that Pleasant Valley wasn't such a bad place to work and raise a family, she continued to urge Grant to move to New York. They argued New Year's Eve in her parents' family room while Jim and Cat were out at a party.

"With your credentials, you could open a practice on Fifth Avenue," Merrilee said. "You'd make tons of money."

"Tons of money isn't the point."

"What *is* the point?"

He had trouble concentrating with her fingers working erotic circles on his earlobe. "I'm a country vet. I like treating agricultural animals and working with farmers. Damned few farmers on Fifth Avenue."

"But thousands of dogs and cats who need you." Her voice was pleading, seductive.

"Dammit, Merrilee." Grant pulled away from her enticing touch and walked the floor in front of the hearth. "I didn't become a vet to treat wealthy women's pampered pooches. I want to spend my life outdoors, not cooped up in some city office or in a home surrounded by skyscrapers, concrete and traffic."

She had risen to her knees on the sofa and fixed her mouth in a pout. "I don't see why you won't at least try it for a few years. You could always come back to Pleasant Valley when Daddy retires."

His temper flared at her selfishness. He struggled for control and tried to look at their situation objectively.

"Look," he said in his most reasonable tone, "you want to be a photographer. Fine. You can shoot pictures anywhere. Ansel Adams and Clyde Butcher are proof of that. You can even shoot pictures in Pleasant Valley, as you discovered last summer. And if I work hard here, we won't be rich, but we'll be able to afford long vacations to anywhere in the world you want to go."

Her pout disappeared and he could tell she was wavering.

"Let me practice here," he said, "and you can decide where we'll spend our time off, places where you can take all the pictures you want. Fair enough?"

She climbed off the sofa and came to him, slipping into his arms with the ease that continually reassured him that they'd been made for each other. "Oh, Grant."

His name on her lips, a sensuous verbal caress, wilted his resistance and made him almost willing to move to New York.

"You know I want to be a famous photographer and I want to be with you. We'll work out something."

He pulled back and tipped her chin to look into her eyes. "Like what?"

"We have months to decide."

She raised her lips to his and the kiss that followed was a prelude to lovemaking that had taken his breath away. He left that night, sated, happy and content that their problem could be resolved.

One day the following summer, after she'd graduated from college, Merrilee was scheduled to meet him at two o'clock on a Saturday afternoon at a dilapidated log cabin set on ten acres that had recently come on the market. Grant had dreams of restoring it and adding a wing that included bedrooms for children and an airy photography studio for Merrilee. He also planned to build a barn and keep his own animals, and there was room for flower and vegetable gardens.

He arrived at the property early and as he surveyed the potential of the place and pictured his life there with Merrilee and their children, he was the happiest he'd been in his life.

That happiness dwindled when Merrilee didn't arrive. The afternoon shadows lengthened, and still she didn't come. He tried calling her cell phone, but heard only recorded messages.

At first he was angry.

Then he grew worried.

Maybe she'd had an accident. Or taken ill. Or been

abducted. Selecting their first home was a milestone in any couple's life. Only some earth-shattering event would prevent Merrilee from keeping her appointment.

He called her house and no one answered. He tried the clinic, but Fran said that Jim was on a call and she hadn't seen Merrilee.

His imagination went into overdrive. He pictured her trapped in her car. Bleeding. Dying. Or lying ill and unconscious on the floor of her home. Or bound and gagged in the back of a serial killer's car. The more he tried to convince himself of a reasonable explanation for her failure to show, the worse his fears grew.

If he lost Merrilee, he didn't know how he would survive. Her sunny smile, her bubbly laugh, her sense of humor and witty conversation had given new meaning to his days and had him yearning for the long, loving nights ahead of them.

He refused to contemplate a world without her.

Grant was ready to call the police and begin his own search when his cell phone rang.

"I'm on my way," Merrilee's breathless voice announced.

Relief cascaded through him. "Are you all right?"

"I'll tell you all about it when I get there."

She arrived ten minutes later in a swirl of red dust, hopped out of her car and ran to him, face shining. "There was a carnival in town."

Relief transformed into anger so overwhelming he saw her through a veil of red. "You've been at a *carnival* while I've been worried out of my mind?"

"I'm sorry." She spoke the words, but she neither appeared nor sounded contrite. She looked radiant. "I should have called, but I was so caught up in taking pictures. Wait till you see the shots I have. You'll understand."

"I tried to call you."

"I forgot to turn on my phone."

"And our appointment? You forgot that, too?" He could feel his blood boiling.

"Of course not. But I kept finding one more shot to take. And the time got away from me."

"Merrilee." He spoke through gritted teeth. "You're three hours late."

She threw him a dazzling look that under other circumstances would have banished his anger, but Grant had spent three hours in agony, worried sick. Usually a patient man, he let his temper blow. "Obviously buying our first home isn't a priority with you."

"It is," she said with what seemed genuine remorse. "But you know how I am when I'm working. I lose all track of time. I said I'm sorry, and I am."

By this time, Grant had worked up enough steam to power Greenville. "Forget it. I'm going home."

He stomped toward his truck.

"But it's still light," Merrilee called after him. "Aren't you going to show me the place?"

Afraid of what he'd say in his current state, he said nothing, climbed into his truck and drove away, leaving Merrilee standing in his dust.

That night, after he'd had time to cool off, he realized that he'd overreacted. Yes, Merrilee should have called him, but Grant could also name a dozen instances when he had become so engrossed in his work that he'd lost track of time. Yes, Merrilee had been wrong, but so had he.

He drove straight to her parents' house to tell her so. Jim had answered the door, his face puzzled. "Sorry, but Merrilee insists she doesn't want to see you."

"I was a jerk," Grant admitted to his friend and partner. "She was late and I overreacted."

"Let her sleep on it," Jim suggested. "I'm sure she'll come around in the morning."

She'd come around all right.

Merrilee was waiting at the clinic the next day when Grant arrived before anyone else. Right there on the front porch, she'd given back his ring.

"I can't marry you, Grant." She wouldn't meet his gaze, fixing her blue eyes on a point past his shoulder.

He felt as if she'd poked him with a cattle prod. "You're kidding, right?"

She shook her head, still avoiding his eyes. "I realized yesterday that my career *is* more important than you, than us. And the prospect of living in Pleasant

Valley suffocates me. I'm moving to New York, as I'd originally planned. I'm sorry."

Before he had a chance to gather his wits to reply, she hurried to her car and pulled away.

Merrilee had left him dazed, as if he'd been clobbered with a two-by-four. When he'd come to his senses again, he'd followed her home, but she had refused to see or to even talk to him before she'd moved out of her parents' home a few weeks later. He'd tried flowers, candy, love letters. He'd even tried to enlist Cat's help, all to no avail. For months after Merrilee's return to New York, she hadn't answered his calls, his letters.

For a long time he'd been angry and blamed her for misleading him. Then he'd finally accepted that she'd been right. If her career was more important than their relationship, she'd done the proper thing. Better a clean break early than a messy divorce later.

But acknowledging that fact hadn't stopped her desertion from hurting like hell. Hadn't stopped him from loving her. And now she was back in Pleasant Valley, albeit not of her own accord.

And she was keeping him waiting again.

"Dr. Nathan," Fran called from the front door.

Grant took a deep breath to calm his anger. "Yes?"

"Your sister just phoned. Merrilee's on her way and should be here in a few minutes."

At least this time Merrilee had bothered to call sooner. The knot of anger loosened in his chest. "Ring Jeff Davidson, please, and tell him I'm running late."

Fran disappeared into the clinic, and Grant, with Gloria at his side, settled on the front steps to wait. An old misgiving surfaced to niggle at his brain. He couldn't shake the conviction he'd had all these years that Merrilee *had* loved him, even more than her career, and that some other reason had been responsible for their breakup. It couldn't have been his brief display of temper. After all, he'd apologized almost immediately, admitting he'd been wrong.

They'd been so compatible, so *right* for each other. And, if she'd really wanted to, she could have pursued her career in Pleasant Valley. He was missing some important piece of the puzzle and he couldn't figure what it was.

The only way he'd ever know the true motive for her desertion was to ask her flat-out. And he intended to, first good chance he had. If he was going to spend the rest of his life without the woman he loved more than breathing, he damned well wanted to know why.

At the sound of an approaching vehicle, he looked up to see Merrilee pulling into the parking lot. She jumped out of her grandmother's car, grabbed her camera bag and hurried toward him.

She started her apology before she reached him.

"I'm really sorry I'm late. I started in plenty of time, but when I went to my car, I had two flats."

She looked so sincerely apologetic, the last vestige of his anger dissipated. "That was bad luck."

"Nothing to do with luck," she said with a shake of her head. "Not according to Jay-Jay. Someone let the air out of my tires on purpose."

Chapter Six

Grant opened the passenger door of the pickup. "Hop in. You can tell me about it on the way."

MJ, knowing he was late for his appointment, hurried onto the passenger seat.

"Somebody purposely let the air out?" Grant motioned Gloria into the rear seat of the cab, then slid behind the wheel. "Jay-Jay's sure?"

MJ nodded. "The pressure in the tires was normal yesterday. He checked them when he charged Nana's battery. Today he double-checked the tires and tested the valves. No punctures or leaks."

"Maybe you dragged the valves against the curb when you parked, releasing the air."

MJ shook her head. "I parked diagonally, smack in front of Jodie's."

A worried frown creased the smoothness of his high forehead. "And nobody saw anything?"

"Downtown's almost deserted this time of year. The

lunch crowd was long gone when I went to my car. I didn't see anyone else on the street."

"Could have been kids."

MJ shrugged. "Kids are in school."

"Maybe. Remember how Jeff Davidson played hooky more often than not?" Grant's frown deepened and he was silent for a moment. "So we don't know if the prank was random or aimed specifically at you."

"It's Nana's car."

"Someone might have seen you in it."

"I vote for random," MJ said. "I don't know anyone who has a grudge against me. Or Nana, either, for that matter."

Brynn's remark about Caroline Tuttle's continued interest in Grant flashed briefly through her mind, but MJ couldn't picture the fastidious Caroline risking breaking a nail or dirtying her hands to flatten tires, not even out of jealousy. Besides, Caroline knew MJ well enough to know a couple of flats wouldn't faze her, much less make her back away from Grant…if she'd still been in love with him.

Which she wasn't, she assured herself.

A new thought hit her. "You don't suppose…nah." She shook her head.

"What?"

"If Ginger Parker knows what I'm up to, she wouldn't be happy." MJ shook her head again. "But as far as I know, she doesn't know I'm in town."

"Maybe somebody's mad at Jodie," Grant suggested.

"Why?"

"Disgruntled customer?"

"I doubt that," MJ said. "I've tasted her food. Any disgruntled employees?"

Grant backed the truck, swung to the entrance, then headed west on the highway. "Jodie's never fired anyone, and Marie and the wait staff seem content. It's probably coincidence that whoever did the deed picked the car in front of her place."

Grant's tone was reasonable, but his expression was fierce. MJ recalled fifteen years earlier, when young Jodie's pregnancy was the hot topic of Pleasant Valley gossip and Jodie herself the brunt of sidelong looks and unkind remarks. MJ had been in middle school, but she clearly remembered how Grant, a high school senior, had championed his little sister. Without striking a blow or raising his voice, he'd drawn a line in the sand. Anyone who crossed it to embarrass or to antagonize Jodie would have to answer to him.

And no one had dared.

He'd been the epitome of a storybook hero, a caped crusader, a knight in shining armor, a white-hatted hero on a white horse, and thirteen-year-old Merrilee had developed a crush on her best friend's older brother that had lasted…

She'd almost thought forever, but MJ had recovered, not only from her first adolescent crush but also from her first real love. Otherwise, how could she have gone away to New York without him? But enclosed in the intimacy of the cab, breathing his scent, hearing his voice, she remembered those old feelings too well.

Gloria's wet nose nuzzled her neck and MJ reached back to pet the dog.

"Meet Gloria," Grant said. "And don't let her size fool you. She's a teddy bear at heart."

"We met this morning in the waiting room. How come you named her Gloria? After an old girlfriend?"

Grant shook his head. "With her sleek head, long lanky legs and regal appearance, she seems bigger than life, like a movie star from the 1930s. Gloria seems to suit her."

MJ hadn't thought for years about Grant's enthusiasm for classic films. "Sounds like you're still fascinated with old movies."

"I watch 'em on cable every chance I get. They remind me of you."

"Me?" His comment puzzled her. "Because they're in black-and-white like so many of my photos?"

"Because we used to watch them together." He shot her a heated glance. "The old stars remind me of you, too."

"I'm not exactly the glitzy-glamour type."

"You're a perfect mix of all the factors that made

Betty Grable, Jean Harlow and Doris Day so appealing."

She felt a blush rising from her collar to her hairline.

"And—" he reached over and ran the back of his hand down her flaming cheek "—you have the advantage of living color."

"Tell me about Jeff," she suggested quickly. She wanted something to take her mind off the man beside her and his compliments that made her uncomfortably warm.

"What's to tell?"

"I'm surprised he's come back."

Grant cast her a look she couldn't read. "Not everyone leaves town for good."

"You know what I mean. Everybody knew his father beat him."

"His father's dead. Left Jeff the family homestead and little else, except bad memories and some nasty scars, physical and emotional."

Remembering the tall, dark and dangerous boy in black leather who'd kept town tongues wagging, she shook her head. "I can't picture Jeff as a farmer."

Grant grinned. "He's not."

MJ frowned in confusion. "But we're going to inspect his stock."

"I'll let Jeff tell you about it." Grant chuckled.

"What are you laughing at?"

He flashed a dazzling smile that brought an unexpected warmth to her insides. "I get a kick out of proving you wrong."

The warmth fizzled into annoyance. "About what?"

"You always say nothing ever changes in Pleasant Valley."

A sudden sadness smothered her. "Guess my parents' breakup is proof against that."

Grant was immediately contrite. "Damn, I'm sorry, Merrilee. I wasn't thinking."

She pushed that unpleasantness away for the moment. "So what's changed with Jeff?"

"Part of it you'll see for yourself. As for the rest, I'll let him tell you."

They drove to the end of the valley where the winding road became a series of switchbacks that worked their way up the mountain. As Merrilee remembered from a rare visit there with her father, the Davidson's property, unlike the fertile farmland of the valley, was mountainous and rocky, its only buildings a rundown house and ramshackle barn. A small terrace, barely big enough for a vegetable patch, a pond and a tiny pasture had been graded out of the eastern slope.

Hiram Davidson, Jeff's father, hadn't made his living from farming, however, but by selling illegal moonshine. He'd hidden his still in the higher reaches of the mountain and the authorities, despite their best efforts, had never discovered it.

Merrilee recalled Jeff as tall and lanky, his long black hair tied back by a leather thong, and looking like he could use a good meal. He'd been arrogant, solitary and had never let anyone close, hadn't had friends that she knew of. Why he'd chosen to return to his unattractive homestead was a mystery.

Especially considering his father.

Hiram had been mean as a snake. His wife, Jeff's mother, had died when Jeff was a baby. Folks in town swore she died in self-defense, unable to withstand the abuse and neglect. But Hiram sober was sweetness and light compared to when he'd been drinking. Brynn's police chief father had locked the scoundrel up for brawling so many times, the department had named a jail cell after him.

"I'm glad we don't have to deal with Hiram," Merrilee said with a shiver of remembrance.

"He's been gone over a year."

"Cirrhosis of the liver?"

Grant shook his head. "Pancreatic cancer."

"So now Jeff owns the family place?"

Grant nodded. "Such as it is."

"Is he still running moonshine?" She pictured the big, noisy Harley Jeff used to ride, its saddlebags filled with mason jars of white lightning, cushioned with moss to keep them from breaking.

"When Hiram died," Grant explained, "Jeff alerted

the Feds, led them to the still, and they destroyed it. He has other plans for the property."

Grant turned off the highway onto a gravel road almost hidden by arching branches of rhododendron heavy with buds among the glossy, dark green leaves. The truck continued to climb through the hardwood forest that towered over the road, obscuring the sun. When Grant pulled into an open clearing, Merrilee blinked, both from sudden sunlight and surprise.

Excitement coursed through her.

"Stop!" she yelled.

Gloria woofed in alarm and Grant slammed on the brakes.

"What?" he asked.

Too absorbed to answer, MJ grabbed her camera and climbed from the car. Late-afternoon sun filtered through the tall leafless trunks and bathed the clearing in an ethereal golden glow. Striations of light and shadow played on the gray weathered boards of the ancient barn, making it appear as if it had been painted by an Impressionist. Working fast before the remarkable light faded, she raised her camera, framed the shot and snapped the building. She repeated the procedure to capture the scene from several angles.

Unaware of anything except the images in her viewfinder, MJ didn't hear anyone approach. As a result, when the light eventually shifted and spoiled the effect, she stopped, slung the camera strap over her shoulder and turned back toward the truck, only to find Grant, Gloria and a familiar-looking stranger barring her way.

"You been living too long in the big city, Merrilee June. From all those pictures you were taking, I'd think you'd never seen a barn before." The man's slow, easy grin softened the sarcasm of his words.

"It's not the barn so much as the light," MJ explained and tried to place the man. "But it's gone now."

He was as tall as Grant, but more muscled. His deep gray eyes were friendly, his posture relaxed. When he ran his hand over his dark hair, close-cropped in military fashion, the sleeve of his T-shirt slipped, revealing a tattoo of the Marine insignia with "Semper Fi" on his bulging bicep.

"Jeff Davidson." The pieces clicked into place. He'd changed so much from the skinny, unkempt, sullen teenager she remembered, she hadn't recognized him at first, even though she'd been expecting to see him. What had thrown her was his smile. In all the years she'd known him, she'd never seen him with a happy expression before today.

"It's been a long time," Jeff said.

MJ tallied in her head. "At least twelve years."

"I'd better get busy." Grant hefted his medical bag. "Where do you want me to start?"

Jeff nodded toward a pasture behind the barn. "The goat herd. I have five new kids."

MJ fell in step with the two men as they rounded the barn, extending her stride to keep up with them. "You're raising goats?"

"Among other things," Jeff said. "I also have three milk cows, five pigs, a flock of chickens and four horses. And ducks."

"What, no partridge in a pear tree?" Merrilee asked.

Jeff didn't answer, but another dazzling smile suggested her teasing pleased him.

"But Grant said you weren't into farming," she added.

"I'm not."

"What's this then?" MJ nodded toward the goats that came running at their approach. "A petting zoo?"

Grant and Jeff exchanged grins.

"You tell her," Grant said. "It's your baby."

Jeff folded his arms on the top rail of the fence and gazed over the enclosure, pride of ownership evident in his expression. "There's still lots to do yet, but when I'm finished, I'll have a boys' ranch."

"A summer camp?" MJ asked, perplexed. Jeff had never struck her as the warm and fuzzy type, especially where children were concerned.

The ex-Marine shook his head. "Year-round. This is a private venture, but I'm working in cooperation with state social services. This—" his gesture took in the barn, pasture, garden and house "—will be a last chance for teenagers who've broken the law. I've hired counselors, including a psychologist, who'll work with them to turn their lives around before they end up behind bars with a criminal record and serious jail time."

"Whew," MJ said. "You have your work cut out for you."

"Work is an understatement," Grant said. "Delinquent teenagers. Man, that takes guts."

"No guts, no glory," Jeff said. "Besides, the Marines taught me to work hard." The unfamiliar smile lighted his face once more. "And to be fearless. Or, at least, to act that way."

"You can't let kids know you're afraid," MJ said with an understanding nod. "They become predators, sniffing blood and moving in to finish you off."

"You a teacher, like your mom?" Jeff asked.

She shook her head. "But I've photographed enough children's parties to learn the little darlings' killer instincts."

Grant had been scrutinizing the herd. "Your goats seem healthy. Let's have a closer look."

He entered the enclosure, kneeled beside the nearest kid, and swooped it up, a tan-and-white bundle that seemed mostly long legs. Cradled in Grant's arms, the kid nuzzled beneath his chin, obviously content.

Jeff peered over Grant's shoulder. "That's Gunny."

"Strange name," MJ observed.

"Named after my gunnery sergeant," Jeff said. "But this little fellow has a much sweeter disposition." Devilment lighted his gray eyes. "Smells better, too."

The men fastened their attention on the animal and MJ quickly lifted her camera. Jeff and Grant, both over six feet tall and well-built, dwarfed the tiny kid, but what made the image most memorable were the tender expressions on the faces of the tough ex-Marine and the practical vet and the reciprocal trust of the animal in their grasp.

While Grant examined and immunized one kid at a time, MJ took several pictures of the young goats gamboling in the pasture. Then the ducklings on the pond, swimming in formation behind their mother, caught her eye and she shot more frames.

She followed Jeff and Grant as the vet inspected each of Jeff's animals, prescribed medication for mastitis for one of the cows, discussed the best feed for the chickens and admired the horses Jeff had recently purchased.

In the horse stall, MJ captured her favorite vignettes of the day. As Grant stood beside the roan mare, rubbing the horse's muzzle, the faint overhead bulb and the last rays of sun streaming through the open doors of the hayloft above created a lighting effect a Dutch Master would have envied. She loved the way the sunlight glinted gold on Grant's thick hair and gave a corresponding sheen to the mare's coat. Grant gazed into the roan's eyes and the horse returned his look with an expression of silent communication. MJ prayed the resulting print would show the gentleness of Grant's touch, the calming message in his gaze as he soothed the horse's nervousness at the presence of strangers.

MJ couldn't help contrasting her own inner turmoil with Grant's serenity. He was obviously at man at peace with himself and with nature, and that tranquillity translated itself to both the people and animals around him. He operated with the rhythms of the seasons, accepting the changes in the earth as easily as he did the cycles of life and death among the animals he treated. Unlike the frenetic rat race of the city dwellers she'd lived among, Grant's pace was deliberate and purposeful, but without hurry, as if he were attuned to God's time. Just being around him soothed her frazzled nerves and momentarily eased the horrendous ache her parents' separation had created in her heart.

Grant was as elemental as the earth, but there was fire there, too, and she saw it now, shining in his eyes when his gaze met hers. She looked away and hurriedly aimed her camera for a throwaway shot, afraid to confront what she recognized in his expression.

Later, when Grant had completed his rounds, they stood in the barnyard in the deepening twilight.

"When are you expecting your first clients?" Grant asked Jeff.

"Not until June," Jeff said, "after construction on the main building is finished."

MJ looked around and saw no structures other than the house and barn. "But you haven't started yet."

"No sweat," Jeff said. "I have a whole crew of former Marines coming next week to help put up a timber-frame building. It'll have a dormitory, a dining hall and big kitchen. We'll be ready in time. Speaking of kitchen, y'all want to stay for supper?"

MJ looked to Grant, hoping he'd say yes. For reasons she couldn't explain, she wasn't looking forward to dining alone with him.

"Thanks, but we've made other plans," Grant said.

"Ah," Jeff said with a knowing expression. "I understand."

"It's not what you think," MJ said quickly.

Amusement tugged at the corners of Jeff's mouth. "And what was I thinking?"

In spite of herself, MJ blushed and almost stumbled over her words in her haste to explain. "Maybe you haven't heard that Grant and I broke our engagement years ago. But we're still friends."

She could have kicked herself the minute the words left her mouth. Why did she feel the need to make explanations to a man she barely knew? And why didn't Grant say anything? He merely stood, watching her with an expression she couldn't read.

"I had heard that," Jeff admitted. "But situations and people change. I'm living proof."

MJ opened her mouth to insist that her situation hadn't changed, but Grant spoke first.

"Call me if you have any problems." He started for the truck.

"Whoa," Jeff called and ran after him. "What do I owe you?"

"It's on the house," Grant said. "If you're willing to risk your neck and sanity taking in juvenile delinquents, providing free vet care is the least I can do."

"You're a good man." Jeff shook his hand.

As the truck pulled away, Jeff's praise rang in MJ's ears. Grant *was* a good man. The best, now that her father had slipped from top place on her list. And also one of the *few* men she actually knew, she reminded herself, except for Randy and Phil, who shared an apartment across the hall from her New York place and were delightfully gay. In her line of work, most men she crossed paths with were either getting married or just turning thirteen years old.

"You knew about Jeff's project?" she asked.

Grant nodded. "He consulted me before purchasing his livestock. He's hoping caring for animals will help instill a sense of responsibility in his teenage clients."

"Bonding with an animal might be the only affection some of these kids have known," MJ said. "I have a friend in New York who takes her Jack Russell terrier to nursing homes. The elderly patients adore him. Dad always said animals are good therapy."

"You took a lot of pictures at Jeff's," Grant observed as he pulled onto the highway.

Satisfaction, something she rarely experienced after a shoot, flooded her. "These are some of the best I've done. They'll make a great start for the book."

"The book's supposed to be about your father," Grant reminded her, "not me."

"I'm going to expand the project to include the whole practice," MJ said.

No way was she going to omit the shots of Grant she'd taken today. Even before printing them, she knew they were extraordinary examples of light and composition. More than photographs, they were true works of art.

"Will your nana approve?"

"As long as I bring Mom and Dad back together, Nana won't care what's in the book." A thought struck her. "But I'm not going to let Nana pay for it."

He took his eyes from the road for a quick glance that revealed his surprise. "You're self-publishing? Isn't that expensive?"

"I don't have the funds to produce the book myself," MJ said. "I'll find an agent to sell it for me."

"With your New York contacts, that shouldn't be hard." Bitterness sharpened his tone. "I'm surprised you don't already have an agent."

She refused to admit that she hadn't considered her work good enough yet to warrant one. But today's shots were different and, as she analyzed why, she realized that the pictures she'd taken in New York had a staged, artificial quality, while what she'd shot at Jeff's farm had a freshness and spontaneity that breathed life into her work.

Nana had always said that things had a way of working out for the best, if one just waited long enough. Earlier, MJ had bemoaned the interruption to her work that her homecoming had caused. Enthusiasm filled her now as she contemplated the possibility that the book Nana had conjured to reunite Jim and Cat might launch MJ's career in ways she'd never imagined.

She'd broken her engagement with Grant to pursue that career, and now, ironically, returning to Pleasant Valley appeared to place the keys to success within reach. But she'd die before she'd admit that to Grant.

"What's for supper?" she asked to change the subject.

"Worried?" His teasing look warmed her and stirred feelings best left buried.

"Maybe you'd better just take me home," she suggested.

He laughed. "Not only worried, but chicken, too. Afraid I'll poison you?"

She was afraid all right, but not of food poisoning.

Watching Grant in action today had reminded her of too many reasons she'd loved him in the past. If she spent much more time with him, she'd be playing with fire.

"Most men aren't exactly renowned for their cooking," she said.

"Yeah, you're right. James Beard, Emeril, Wolfgang Puck, Bobby Flay, they're all famous for something besides their skill in a kitchen."

"You watch the Food Channel?" she asked in amazement.

"You think vets are only allowed Animal Planet?"

"I never guessed you're into cooking."

"Somebody has to feed me." The look he gave her glowed with enough heat to boil water. "There's a lot about me you don't know, Merrilee June."

Better that she didn't learn, she assured herself. Better that she not place herself in the intimacy of Grant's home, the home he'd originally intended to share with her and their children. The prospect panicked her.

"You were kind to invite me this morning, but I don't want to inconvenience—"

"I've thought of you in a lot of ways, but never as an inconvenience."

The innuendo in his voice only increased her agitation. "I'm exhausted, Grant. Please take me home."

"Afraid to be alone with me?"

"No!" she lied.

"Good. I'll feed you, then take you home. Besides, I want to show off the house. It's changed a lot since the last time you saw it."

If she continued to object, he might sense the reason behind her reluctance and her pride couldn't allow that, so she abandoned her protests. But she had shut the door on a life with Grant long ago. Tonight she'd make certain it remained locked and barred.

As they neared Grant's place, her curiosity stirred. The one glimpse she'd had of the house that fateful summer day had revealed a log cabin, ready to collapse in a strong wind, nothing like the picture-perfect home her parents owned. She'd hated the house the moment she saw it, but not liking the place had been the least of her problems that day.

The following morning she'd broken their engagement, certain she'd done the right thing. Even though she'd missed Grant terribly, she'd never doubted she'd made the best decision.

The last thing on earth she wanted was for Grant to prove her wrong.

Chapter Seven

Nearing his house, Grant flicked on his turn signal and pressed the brake. As he swung the truck toward the driveway, the headlights swept a split-rail fence and two stone pillars at the entrance.

"Is this the same place?" Disbelief colored Merrilee's voice.

"Don't tell me I've surprised you twice in one day," Grant said with a chuckle.

"What happened to the red dirt road with a gazillion potholes?"

He'd used the money he'd intended to spend on an extra wing, the one with the children's bedrooms and Merrilee's studio, to pave the driveway. "I've made lots of changes."

The drive wound up the hillside through the forest. At the last curve, the house was visible through the trees. Every time Grant saw it, satisfaction at his achievement overflowed.

A green-metal roof replaced the rotting shingles. He'd rechinked the logs, repaired the sagging porch columns and installed missing rails. He'd also torn down the crumbling brick chimney and rebuilt it with fieldstone he'd gathered off his own land.

Working on the house had kept him sane. When Merrilee had broken their engagement, fled to New York and refused to speak to him, when she hadn't answered his letters or returned his phone calls, Grant had refused to yield to heartbreak.

He'd held on to anger instead.

Every nail hammered, every board sawn, every rock mortared had provided a slow release for turmoil that had nowhere else to go. He'd loved Merrilee too deeply to vent his rage at her. And he'd been mad as hell at himself for falling so hard for a woman who'd insisted from the start she'd be pulling up stakes and leaving town. In his conceit, he'd believed he could change her mind. For almost a year he'd been convinced that he *had* changed her mind. Then, when their relationship went south and Merrilee headed north, he'd felt lost, disoriented.

And hopping mad.

The house had saved him. When he hadn't been working as a vet, he'd spent every spare moment on the place, falling into bed in the wee hours of the morning so exhausted that he'd slept hard in spite of his emotional pain.

Two years later he'd expended his anger, finished his house and gained a tenuous inner peace. What he hadn't had, however, were answers. Even if only for the sake of his ego, he intended to find out tonight why Merrilee had misled him and whether she'd really loved him, loved him still, as his gut insisted, or if she'd simply been pretending all along.

He parked the truck on the flagstone landing he'd built in front of the house. Welcoming golden light poured from the windows onto the porch and low-voltage lamps illuminated the surrounding gardens and up-lighted the ancient hickory in the front yard.

"The lights are on," Merrilee said. "Is somebody here?"

Grant shook his head. "Photoelectric cells."

He didn't add how he hated coming home to a dark house. Bad enough that the place was empty, but stepping alone into darkness was too depressing.

Gloria whimpered in the back seat.

"Don't worry, girl," he consoled the dog in his most soothing voice. "You'll get fed."

To Merrilee, he added, "I'm glad her appetite is back. When I first found her, she'd given up the will to live. Wouldn't eat or drink."

Merrilee reached into the rear seat and scratched Gloria's ear. "She was hurt that badly?"

"Her injuries were severe, but her spirit had taken the biggest hit."

"How did you perk her up?"

"I kept her with me round-the-clock. Literally carried her to the clinic every day where I had a special bed for her in my office. At night, she slept next to me. It took a while to earn her trust, and once I did, she wouldn't let me out of her sight. She suffers from separation anxiety now if I leave her, but I'm hoping the new medication helps."

"I do, too. She's a sweet dog."

Gloria stuck her head between the seats and licked Merrilee's cheek. To Merrilee's credit, she didn't flinch or pull away.

"She likes you." Grant bit his tongue to keep from adding how much he liked Merrilee, in spite of his best efforts not to.

He climbed out, with Gloria on his heels, circled the truck and met Merrilee as she was jumping down from the high seat.

"I hope you like soup," he said.

"You're opening cans." She confronted him with an I-told-you-so grin. "You should be ashamed. I knew you couldn't cook."

"Wanna bet?" He took the porch stairs two at a time,

unlocked the door and opened it wide. "Step inside and take a deep breath."

He followed Merrilee indoors and tried to see the room through her eyes. He'd converted the lower floor into a great room that contained living and dining areas and the kitchen. A spacious bedroom loft above the kitchen gave it a low, intimate feel, but the living and dining room ceiling soared two stories high with exposed, ancient beams.

Except for the fireplace, the gable end of the room was a wall of glass that overlooked a fieldstone terrace and the adjacent mountains. A deep leather sofa, a comfy recliner and an antique wooden rocker with a seat of woven rushes were grouped around the stone hearth. Not anywhere close to the Ritz, but homey and comfortable, a place a man could relax in after a hard day.

He crossed the room and set a match to the logs and kindling already laid.

"What is that delicious smell?"

Merrilee wasn't admiring the decor. She stood just inside the door, eyes closed, sniffing deeply.

"Canned soup?" Grant teased.

"No way." She opened her eyes and looked at him. "What with worrying over Mom and Dad, I've hardly eaten in two days. That aroma brings my appetite back. Please tell me what you're cooking is as good as it smells."

"Better. Let me take your coat."

She shrugged hurriedly out of her jacket and handed it to him. He hung it on a coatrack by the front door and turned to discover she'd moved to the middle of his kitchen.

She surveyed the Shaker-style maple cabinets, granite countertops and stainless-steel appliances with interest. "This looks like something out of *Home and Garden*. I could fit my New York kitchen in here five times and still have room for a square dance."

He didn't speak for fear of exposing the emotion rising in his throat. He'd dreamed about her in his house, his kitchen, his bed, more times than he cared to admit. To see her actually here made him happy but also resurrected his old anger.

Gloria's whimper of hunger jarred him out of his thoughts and he joined Merrilee in the kitchen and poured the dog's evening ration of kibble into her dish.

Finally trusting his voice not to break, he said, "Supper will be ready as soon as I warm the bread."

He turned on the broiler, took a package of Texas Toast from the freezer and placed the pieces on a baking sheet.

Merrilee arched an eyebrow. "You don't bake your own?"

Grant nodded to the bread-making machine on the kitchen island. "If you want to wait a couple hours to eat."

Gloria was wolfing down kibble with intermittent moans of delight. Merrilee pointed to the dog. "I think I'm as hungry as she is."

"Store-bought bread it is, then." He placed the toast under the broiler. "Silverware and napkins are in the island drawer, if you don't mind setting the table, please."

For the next few minutes they worked in companionable silence. Grant tossed a salad with ready-cut greens from a bag and added slices of tomato and Bermuda onion. In a few weeks he'd have lettuce from his own garden, but the weather was too cold yet for planting outdoors. He ladled soup from the Crock-Pot into handmade crockery bowls and placed the hot bread in a basket.

Merrilee stole a piece of lettuce from the salad, set two places at the round antique-oak farm table, then helped carry dishes from the kitchen.

The tranquil domesticity wrenched at his heart and made him face the fact that he'd built this house as much for Merrilee as himself, keeping alive the hope that someday she'd come back and share it with him.

And now she had.

But she was only here for supper, he reminded himself. Tomorrow morning her place at the table would be empty once again.

"Dig in," he said.

She took a mouthful of soup and closed her eyes as

if savoring the flavors. She chewed, swallowed and asked, "What is this? It's wonderful."

"Portuguese stone soup."

"You got the recipe from Jodie, I'll bet." Merrilee took another spoonful.

Grant shook his head. *"Bon appetit."*

"The magazine?" She cast him a skeptical glance. "Don't tell me you have a subscription."

"Fran saw the recipe and made me a copy. Not everyone in South Carolina lives off cornbread, fried chicken and black-eyed peas."

"Not many make soup with pepperoni, either. This is incredible."

He was glad to see her eating again. Maybe a good meal would put some color back in her cheeks and help her sleep. The smudges of fatigue under her eyes worried him. She'd taken her father's betrayal hard, and with her innate mix of tenacity and impulsiveness, she clearly intended to mend her parents' marriage single-handedly. Grant hoped she wasn't in for more heartache.

She's caused you plenty, so why should you care? After all, what goes around comes around.

Grant hoped not. He was angry because things hadn't worked out between them, but he didn't want Merrilee hurt. He loved her too much. He tried to analyze his feelings for the umpteenth time, hoping that if he understood the emotions, he could free himself from them.

She had grown more beautiful with age, but Merrilee would always be much more than a gorgeous face and a knock-out body. She exuded enthusiasm for life and she tried to capture the thrills of living in her photographs. He'd watched her in action this afternoon and noted the shots she'd taken. Her photographs would be more than pretty pictures. They would have depth and emotion, like Merrilee herself. She cared deeply about causes because she cared deeply about people.

So why hadn't she cared about him?

"Grant?"

Her voice jerked him from his thoughts. He'd been lost in them so long, he hadn't noticed that Merrilee had finished her meal.

"More soup?" he asked.

She shook her head. "No, thanks. I was asking about Brittany. I didn't have a chance to talk to Jodie about her this afternoon. How is my goddaughter?"

Grant thought for a moment before answering, wanting to share his concerns about his niece but not wanting to betray his sister's confidences.

"She's growing up," he hedged. "She's already taller than her mother."

"And only fourteen. If she keeps growing, maybe she'll be a model."

Model wasn't a word he associated with Brittany, except as a model pain in the ass. He kept his features neutral, resisting the scowl that thoughts of his niece usually generated.

"Whatever you do," he warned, "don't try to give her advice, on careers or anything else. She's going through her adolescent rebellion stage. Not even reverse psychology works on her now."

"She's not causing Jodie problems?"

Grant tried not to swear under his breath. Merrilee was already worried enough about her parents. She didn't need to add Brittany to the list.

He forced a smile. "Not anything Jodie can't handle. Right now they're negotiating clothing styles, body piercings and tattoos."

Merrilee sighed and shook her head. "I guess the days of ruffled pink dresses and patent-leather shoes are gone for good."

"You got that right. Now it's ratty jeans and T-shirts, in any color as long as it's black."

"I can't believe Brittany's a teenager," Merrilee said with a sigh. "She makes me feel ancient."

Grant laughed at that idea. Merrilee had the kind of spirit that would be eternally young. "Maybe you should sit by the fire, granny, and doze while I do dishes."

"Granny!" She feigned indignation. "I can work circles around an old guy like you any day."

Glad to see Merrilee's sense of humor revived, he suggested, "Then I should sit by the fire and let you clean up."

Merrilee looked thoughtful. "That's fair. You did the cooking."

"Letting my guest do all the work would give Southern hospitality a black eye. Can't have you carrying that tale back north."

"Then you scrape and I'll load the dishwasher?"

"Deal." He rose and began clearing the table.

MERRILEE WATCHED Grant work with the smooth, efficient movements of a man at home in the kitchen. His actions triggered a memory and she knew instantly who he reminded her of.

Her father.

Every night for as long as she'd lived at home, her father had helped her mother clear the table, load the dishwasher and clean the kitchen. Her parents had made the chore seem more like fun than work. Sometimes they'd sung old tunes from the sixties and improvised dance steps. They'd even had soapsuds fights that ended in peals of laughter and soaked clothing.

Other nights, when her dad was concerned over a critically ill animal or her mother worried about a problem student, they worked silently, communicating only with an occasional touch, an understanding glance or a brief kiss. Most often, however, they'd simply shared the mundane details of their day with an intimacy Merrilee had envied. She'd longed to have someone of her own to share that kind of closeness with.

Now with Ginger Parker in the picture, her parents might never do dishes together again. Her family could be shattered for good.

That prospect hit her like a sledgehammer and she gasped for breath.

"Hey." Grant rinsed his hands, dried them and reached for her. "You okay?"

The pain had taken her breath. She shook her head, because she couldn't speak. In the next instant she was consumed by great, gulping sobs that ripped from the depths of her body.

Grant scooped her into his arms, carried her into the living room and settled her on his lap in the antique rocker. Smoothing her hair, he held her close and rocked her gently until her crying subsided. His embrace warmed her, his voice calmed her, but nothing he did could close the void or pull her back from the precipice where she watched her family disintegrate into nothingness.

When she finally regained control, she pulled away to find the front of his shirt soaked by her tears.

"Sorry." She attempted to rise.

He held her fast. "Don't apologize. I understand."

She gazed into his eyes and saw the flickering light from the fireplace reflected in the molten bronze of his pupils. "How can you know what I'm feeling? Your family's all in one piece."

A smile tinged with sadness tugged at the corners of his mouth. "My parents are together, but I lost my family when I lost you."

She didn't want to hear this. She was too vulnerable and those old wounds she'd worried about were beginning to ache.

This time she did push away and he let her go. Wiping her damp cheeks with the back of her hands, she moved to the recliner on the opposite side of the hearth, hoping for invulnerability with distance.

Safely out of his reach, she cast about for a topic, any subject that would make conversation safe again and divert her attention from the love—and sadness—shining in his eyes. One look at him, however, and her mind went blank, leaving her speechless.

"Why?" he asked.

She pretended to misunderstand. "I guess I wouldn't accept the possibility of Mom and Dad splitting for good until tonight."

He shook his head. "You know what I mean. Why did you break our engagement?"

She suppressed the urge to flee into the night, away from the warmth and security of this house that would have been theirs, away from the man who loved her. How could she possibly explain why she'd abandoned someone she had loved more than life when she couldn't fully understand it herself?

"We were all wrong for each other," she said.

"Liar." Anger joined the love in Grant's expression and his fierceness made him even more attractive.

"There's no point in rehashing this," she said with a shake of her head.

"Rehash?"

At the volume and force of that single word, the wolfhound lifted her head from her bed by the fire, ears alert, her muscles tensed, eyes anxious. Gloria crept from the bed and lay at Grant's feet.

"You never explained in the first place!" Grant shouted. "And God knows, I asked. But you wouldn't return my calls or answer my letters."

Guilt racked her. MJ hadn't answered because she hadn't known what to say six years ago, didn't know now. She shoved to her feet. "It's ancient history. Will you please take me home?"

"Not until I have an answer." His low, quiet voice disturbed her more than when he'd shouted.

She sank back into her chair. "I don't *know* the answer."

"You broke our engagement and don't even know why?" Astonishment was evident in his voice, his eyebrows shot up in disbelief and a deep red flushed the strong angles of his cheeks.

She remembered the last time she'd watched Grant's temper flare, at this very house the day before she'd broken their engagement. And she remembered, too, even though it was cliché, that he truly was more handsome when he was angry.

"I told you why a moment ago and you called me a liar," she snapped.

"How can you say we're all wrong for each other after what we shared?"

His voice and face displayed a mix of anger and sadness again, evoking a tenderness she fought to crush. "I need to go," she insisted.

"Give me one example, just one, of how we're wrong for each other," he demanded, "then I'll take you home."

"We fight. Like we're doing now."

His jaw dropped. "And fighting voids everything else?"

"It's not a good indicator," she said defensively. "I never once saw my parents fight."

"Well, they're certainly the poster kids for marital bliss." His sarcasm stung.

At her master's sharp tone, the dog cowered at his feet, flattened her ears and whimpered.

Grant was instantly remorseful, but toward Gloria,

MJ realized, not her. He knelt at the dog's side, stroked her gently and spoke soothingly until the wolfhound appeared to relax.

MJ didn't want to distress the poor animal any more than Grant did, so she tried to keep her voice calm. "It wasn't just the fights. You and I wanted different things."

"Not that different."

"You loved this house. I hated it."

He jerked his head up in surprise. "You did? I didn't know."

"It was a shambles, filthy and falling down. And you expected me to live here. I didn't have your vision for what it could be."

"You should have told me."

"It was more than this place. I love the city. You love the country."

"You thought we could work out the location problem."

She shook her head. "I was wrong. We took forever to decide when to marry, where to honeymoon. And then there was this house and your anger. I was scared."

"Of me?"

His amazement would have been comical if the memories hadn't been so painful.

"Of us."

The truth hit her like a runaway truck. She had refused to recognize her fear before, had always insisted, even to herself, that her career was the reason she'd left Grant.

With Gloria calmed, Grant returned to his chair. Bewilderment shone in his eyes, his forehead wrinkled in a frown. "Scared of us? I don't get it."

"We had too many negatives working against us," MJ admitted.

"But they were outweighed by positives. At least, I thought they were."

"I kept thinking of my parents. They never fought and they always agreed on everything. I wanted a marriage like theirs."

"And look where it got them." The sarcasm had crept back into his voice.

"Which proves my point," MJ said. "If my parents, who had the perfect marriage, couldn't stay together, what hope would there have been for us?"

He shook his head, his eyes sad. "I can't believe we see things so differently."

"You've just proved my point again," she said softly.

"So love had nothing to do with it?" His gaze bored into her.

She looked away. "It couldn't have been the kind of love that lasts, or we wouldn't have had so many differences."

He started to say more, then seemed to think better

of it. His expression softened with a tenderness that created an ache beneath her breastbone.

"It's late," he said, "and you're exhausted. I'll drive you home."

"But Nana's car's at the clinic."

"I'll pick you up in the morning and take you to get it." He turned to Gloria. "Want to go for a ride, girl?"

The dog, her earlier anxiety forgotten, leaped to her feet and raced to the door.

THE TRIP INTO TOWN was a silent one. MJ, afraid of renewing their previous discussion, said nothing. Grant kept his eyes on the road and his thoughts to himself.

Try as she might, she couldn't shake the certainty that their discussion hadn't settled anything, at least not as far as Grant was concerned.

When they reached her parents' house, she didn't recall leaving the porch light on, but was glad she had. Facing going inside without her parents waiting was hard enough. At least the glowing porch light provided a smidgen of cheer.

She opened her door and climbed out, hoping to say goodbye at the curb, but Grant hopped out, too, and caught up with her.

"Thanks for dinner," she said as Grant walked her to the door. "And for the afternoon. I'll show you the pictures once I've printed them."

She turned to unlock the door.

"Wait."

He caught her by surprise, pulling her into his arms and crushing his mouth to hers. Desire shot through her, mowing down reason and resistance like a tsunami hitting a beach. Her brain shut down and muscle memory took over, recalling in intimate detail every time their bodies had touched. Without thinking, she twined her arms around his neck, strained on tiptoe and arched against him. As in one of a thousand dreams she'd had over the past years, she opened her lips to his, breathed in his scent of sunshine and spicy aftershave and felt the cordoned muscles of his arms tighten and lift her off her feet.

A moan of pleasure escaped from the back of her throat. Another emotion, stronger and more powerful, burst from the shadows of her heart where it had lain trapped and buried for so long. It joined with her desire. She ached with love as she savored the taste, the touch, the essence of him once again. And recognized the black, gaping hole his absence in her world had caused.

Another part of her clamored for her attention, fed her fears, sounded the alarm bells in her mind, but the power of Grant's embrace, his mesmerizing kiss, blocked all other sensations.

Without success, she tried to break away, to focus on

their earlier discussion, on all the reasons they were wrong for one another, but with his strong hands kneading the muscles of her back, his breath mingling with hers, his lips shooting heat throughout her body, she couldn't think. Couldn't breathe. Couldn't do anything but kiss him back with every fiber of her being.

Grant twined his fingers through her hair. Then he lifted his head and stared at her in the yellow glow of the porch light, but didn't loosen his grip. His eyes sparked with fire and when he finally spoke, his voice was raw, as if he'd spent the last hour screaming.

"Now tell me we're all wrong for each other. I dare you."

"I—"

She was saved from answering by the sudden opening of the front door. Grant released her and they turned to find her father standing on the threshold.

"Daddy!" she sputtered in surprise.

In the lighted hall behind him sat a stack of luggage partially obscured by a pile of clothes on hangers.

"Merrilee June?" Her father's face showed both strain and astonishment.

She straightened her clothes with a self-conscious gesture, knowing her lips were still swollen from Grant's kiss, her cheeks flaming with excitement.

Fighting through the haze of desire, she realized that her father was home and had brought his belongings with him. Her hope for the survival of her parents' marriage soared.

"What are you doing home, princess?"

If the situation had been less serious, she would have laughed at his befuddled expression. "Guess I could ask you the same thing, Daddy."

Chapter Eight

Early the next morning Merrilee must have been watching for Grant from the porch, because she sprinted down the front walk before he'd even pulled his truck to the curb. His pulse accelerated at the sight of her, with her honey-blond hair tousled by the wind, cheeks flushed from the cold, her stride graceful and athletic.

He grinned when he realized what he was thinking. *She doesn't run like a girl.*

But she was definitely one hundred percent female and the only woman he'd ever loved. If he'd had any doubts—and he hadn't—last night's kiss would have destroyed them. Having Merrilee back in Pleasant Valley and in his arms made him happier than he'd been in over six years.

"Calm down," he ordered Gloria, who'd barked in greeting at the sight of Merrilee.

As the wolfhound complied with her characteristic eagerness to please, he reached across the seat to open the passenger door.

Merrilee slid inside. "Thanks for coming."

"No problem. Your dad have an emergency?"

The previous night, knowing Merrilee needed to talk privately with her father, Grant had left almost immediately after Jim had opened the door. She'd called to Grant that her dad would drive her to the clinic this morning to pick up her grandmother's car.

Last night, Grant had been glad for the reprieve, giving him time to cool off, slow down. In his frustration, he'd pushed too hard with both his kiss and his questions.

But he'd also learned two very important facts. First, that Merrilee loved him. They had *shared* that kiss and he'd been blown away by her response. Her hunger had matched his in intensity. Good thing Jim had opened the door when he had or Grant might have carried their embrace to its logical conclusion, something Merrilee wasn't ready for, not emotionally anyway.

Because the second fact Grant had learned yesterday was that Merrilee's love for him scared her to death. With her parents' so-called perfect marriage crumbling in front of her eyes, she was more terrified than ever of being hurt. If Grant intended to convince her that loving him was a safe bet, that he wasn't going to break her heart, he'd have to back off and go slow.

Today, in the bright, clear light of morning, while his heart urged him to grab her and hold her close, reason insisted he wait until she'd come to terms with whatever was happening between her parents before pressing his own case.

But the knowledge that Merrilee still cared, even though she was too frightened of her feelings to admit them, gave him hope.

And fueled his patience.

For now he'd give her the emotional distance she needed. The last thing he wanted was to spook her into taking off for New York again.

Beside him, Merrilee scrunched her face into a frown. "Dad was gone when I woke up. Left a note on the kitchen counter that he'd see me later, but it didn't say where he was going."

"Back to Ginger?"

"Maybe." She shuddered. "Frankly, I don't have a clue what's happening."

Grant put the truck in gear and pulled onto the street. "Last night it looked like Jim was moving back home."

Merrilee's smile held such sadness, Grant was tempted again to stop the truck and wrap his arms around her. But he didn't.

Play it safe, he reminded himself. *Let her get her bearings again.*

"When I first saw Dad last night, I thought for sure he'd left Ginger," Merrilee said.

"He hasn't?"

"From what little I talked to him, Dad sounds as infatuated as ever. He's not himself. He's…detached. It's like some alien has taken over his body. Like in that old sci-fi movie where space beings come to earth, leave their pods under the beds and use humans for hosts."

"Did you check under his bed?" he teased. "For alien pods?"

She smiled, as he'd hoped, but her eyes were teary and her lower lip trembled.

"Did he talk about leaving your mom?"

Merrilee took a deep breath, as if struggling for control, and shook her head. "That was the weirdest part. He acted as if what he's doing is *normal*. I wanted to ask how he can look at himself in the mirror after the way he's treated Mom, but I remembered Nana's warnings."

"Good girl." Grant was well aware of his partner's stubborn side.

Merrilee erupted in an indignant snort, an unladylike noise Sally Mae would not approve of. "Dammit, what I really wanted was to shake him and scream, but I knew I wouldn't get through to him. It's as if that woman has him under some kind of spell."

Frustration gnawed at Grant. He wanted to help make things right again in the Stratton family, but, in a case like this, there wasn't anything he could do, except wait for Jim to come to his senses.

"If your dad's still—" Grant fumbled for the right word "—interested in Ginger, why did he bring his stuff home?"

"That was Ginger's idea."

"She kicked him out?"

"I wish."

"So he's not home for good?"

Merrilee took another deep breath and exhaled slowly, her sigh so poignant it stabbed through Grant like a serrated blade. "According to Dad, Ginger said they shouldn't live together. Yet. Not while Dad's on the rebound from Mom."

"'Rebound'?" Grant stared at Merrilee in astonishment, then forced his attention back to the winding road. "She breaks up his marriage, then complains he's on the rebound? The woman's a fruitcake on wheels."

"And Dad's not far behind. He thinks she's wonderful, her being so concerned about their future together. He almost glows when he mentions her name. It made me sick to see him like that."

"Let's hope his coming home turns out to be a good thing," Grant said. "Familiar surroundings will help him regain his reason."

"Don't count on it. I woke up in the middle of the night. The lights were on downstairs when I went to the kitchen for something to drink, and Dad was in the family room on the computer."

"His guilty conscience keeping him awake?" Grant suggested.

Merrilee shook her head. "He didn't hear me come in, so I watched for a few minutes. He was on the Web, surfing sites that sell jewelry. Very expensive jewelry. As soon as he realized I was in the room, he switched off his monitor."

Grant frowned. He'd hoped Merrilee would get some much-needed rest last night, but the faint circles remained under her eyes. Jim had to be at least *half* crazy not to see what he was doing to his daughter.

"You think he was buying a peace offering for your mom?"

"He didn't mention Mom once last night, and he seemed really disappointed about Ginger asking him to move out." She set her jaw and her blue eyes glittered with anger. "I think she's playing hard to get. If he's buying jewelry, it's for her."

Grant puzzled over his partner's bizarre behavior, so uncharacteristic of the integrity of the man he'd worked with for years.

"The woman's so blatantly manipulative," Merrilee said with disgust, "you'd think Dad would see it."

"Not necessarily. I had a wise old professor in veterinary school who gave us a talk about objectivity. His example was simplistic but drove home the point. Hold your finger about a foot in front of your nose."

"Why?"

"Humor me, okay?"

Merrilee shrugged, lifted her right index finger about twelve inches in front of her face and stared at it. "Now what?"

"Can you see it?"

"Of course. It's right before my eyes."

Grant slowed for a curve where a bridge crossed the river. "Now place that same finger on the tip of your nose."

"I assume there's a point to this."

"How well can you see your finger now?" From the corner of his eye, he watched her twist her head, trying for a better look.

"Hardly at all."

"That was the professor's point. The closer you are to a situation, the harder it is for you to see it clearly. That's what's happening with Jim. If he could stand back and take a good look at himself, he'd see how wrong and ridiculous his behavior is."

Merrilee scowled. "I wonder if Ginger knows this and is keeping him off balance on purpose?"

"My guess is she's had lots of practice with her game."

"Brynn thinks so, too. She's checking with the police in the town Ginger came from."

Grant slowed to turn into the clinic parking lot. "Brynn has good instincts. I'll be curious to see what she turns up."

Grant parked the truck next to Merrilee's grandmother's car.

"Thanks again for the ride." Merrilee climbed out. "I'll see if Dad's here."

"No problem."

Wishing he could do more than provide transportation and moral support, Grant, with Gloria beside him, followed her inside.

Fran was straightening magazines in the waiting room before the first clients arrived. "I declare, humans make a bigger mess in here than the animals do."

"Is Daddy around?" Merrilee asked.

"He's at Mrs. Weatherstone's," Fran said. "He left a message on the office machine."

Grant frowned. "Itty-Bitty?"

"Who's Itty-Bitty?" Merrilee asked.

"A teacup chihuahua," Grant explained, "Old Mrs. Weatherstone's only companion since her husband died. You remember her?"

Merrilee nodded. "She sold her husband's fix-it shop to Jodie after he died."

"The woman's crazy about that dog," Grant said. "It's a feisty little thing, and with her loving care it's lived well beyond its life expectancy."

"Much to its owner's delight," Fran added, "especially since she has no children or grandchildren to keep her company in her old age."

"And Itty-Bitty's sick?" Merrilee asked.

Fran nodded, her face sad. "The dog had a stroke during the night."

Grant closed his eyes briefly, aware of the implications.

"Mrs. Weatherstone called Dr. Stratton at home," Fran explained.

"I didn't hear our phone ring," Merrilee said. "She must have called him on his cell."

"According to his message," Fran said, "he's been there since 4:00 a.m. The poor little dog's terminal, but Dr. Stratton said he'll stay as long as necessary."

Grant understood. "Unless the dog's in pain, Mrs. Weatherstone will hold on to her little friend as long as she can. And Jim will stay with them until the end, then make sure Mrs. Weatherstone isn't alone afterward."

"Poor Itty-Bitty," Merrilee murmured. "And poor Mrs. Weatherstone."

Grant nodded in agreement. "She'll take losing the dog hard. It's all the family she has left."

Fran returned to the reception desk.

Merrilee spoke softly. "Thank goodness, Dad hasn't lost all sense. I'm glad he's staying there."

"That he still has his compassion is a good sign." Grant gave Merrilee's hand a squeeze.

The front door of the waiting room flew open and Brittany barged in.

Grant dropped Merrilee's hand and, as usual, stopped

himself from rolling his eyes at his niece's strange attire.

She wore skintight black jeans, a long-sleeved clinging black knit top with a plunging neckline, clunky black shoes and at least three sets of earrings in the only holes Jodie had allowed so far in her daughter's unending battle for more piercings.

Despite her dark, heavy eyeliner, makeup that made her pale skin even whiter, and deep red, almost-black lipstick, Brittany was still a pretty girl. Except for her perpetual pout. Her long, blond hair was naturally platinum, her eyes a startling green, and she had her mother's high cheekbones and forehead. Jodie had been mischievous and funny as a teenager until Brittany's arrival had forced her to grow up too fast. Where his niece had inherited her sullen disposition, Grant hadn't a clue.

Brittany stopped short when she spotted Merrilee, slid her gaze away as if Merrilee wasn't there, and looked at him. "Hey, Uncle Grant."

Grant fought and lost to control his irritation at her bad manners. "Aren't you going to speak to your godmother?"

Merrilee, her face beaming with affection, stepped toward Brittany, arms extended for a hug. "You're two inches taller than the last time I saw you."

"Well, duh." Brittany sidestepped, avoiding Merrilee's attempt at an embrace. "Growing up is what kids do, isn't it?"

"That's no way to talk," Grant snapped at the girl. "Your mother taught you better manners."

Merrilee raised her hands and flashed Grant a warning with her eyes. "It's okay. She's right. I was stating the blooming obvious."

In spite of Merrilee's disclaimer, Grant could tell Brittany had hurt her feelings, and the last thing Merrilee needed right now was more hurt. Jim Stratton had inflicted enough pain on her already.

"What are you doing here so early?" Merrilee asked Brittany.

Brittany was sullenly unresponsive until she caught Grant's warning glare.

"I work every Saturday," she said, as if speaking was an imposition. "I walk the dogs, clean kennels and the stable." She tossed her hair back with affected nonchalance. "Mom won't have me at the café. She's afraid I'll gross out the customers."

"That's not true," Grant said with more patience than he felt. "You wanted to work here because you like animals."

"Whatever," Brittany said with a bored shrug. "Can I go now?"

If his niece was trying to rile him, Grant refused to give her the satisfaction of knowing she'd succeeded. "We're boarding a pair of cocker spaniels. How about walking them first?"

With a sigh that suggested the task was beneath her, Brittany clumped out of the waiting room through the door that led to the boarding kennels.

"Whew," Merrilee said. "When did that happen?"

"What?"

"The attitude the size of New York."

Grant shook his head. "Jodie says it's a teen thing. I guess they all go through it." He worried about Brittany's moody rebelliousness, but he didn't want to add to Merrilee's problems by admitting it. "She'll outgrow it."

"Before somebody takes offense and punches her in her very pretty nose, I hope." Merrilee smiled, but her expression was forced and didn't cover the hurt in her eyes.

"I'm making rounds this morning," Grant said. "Want to come along and take more pictures?"

Merrilee shook her head. "I should check on Nana. Then I'll drive into Asheville to visit Mom."

"Have supper with me tonight."

She shook her head again.

"I thought you liked my cooking."

"I do. But I want to be at home in case I have a chance to talk with Dad."

The urge to protect her, whether from her father's indiscretions or his niece's rudeness, consumed him.

She seemed to sense his feelings. "I'm a big girl, Grant. I can take care of myself."

But I want to take care of you.

He bit back the words, suddenly overwhelmed by the obstacles that faced him. Bringing Jim Stratton to his senses, improving Brittany's attitude and conquering Merrilee's fears of loving him would all take patience and time.

He had the patience.

He could only pray that time was on his side before Merrilee fled back to New York and out of reach.

"Drive carefully," he said. "And call me if you need me."

His hopes lifted when she rose on tiptoe and planted a fleeting kiss on his cheek. "Thanks. For everything."

Before he could respond, she hurried out the door.

MJ SPENT THE NEXT FEW days in a fog, forcing her mind and body through the motions of normal life.

Twice during that time, she visited Nana and today was the second time she'd met her mother for lunch on the Asheville campus.

Sitting in a restaurant booth across from her mom and watching her toy with her food broke MJ's heart. Her beautiful mother was wasting away before her eyes. Cat had dropped at least ten pounds, her luxuriant hair had lost its sheen, her usually erect posture drooped and the sparkle in her eyes had dimmed.

She perked up briefly when MJ told her that Jim had

moved back home, but her spirits dipped again when MJ explained the reason behind his return.

"I'm worried sick about him," her mother said.

"Worried?" MJ asked in surprise. "Aren't you angry?"

Her mother's sad smile twisted her heart. "That, too. But this isn't like him. Something's wrong."

"Yeah," MJ said with a grimace, "a terminal case of raging testosterone. Maybe I should slip saltpeter into his food."

"Or arsenic in hers." Cat refused to speak Ginger Parker's name, as if by not acknowledging it, she could make the woman nonexistent.

"Jodie and I have already considered and rejected that option."

Anger flashed across her mother's face. "Jim's a married man, a father. What kind of woman thinks it's okay to break up a family?"

"One who doesn't value family life and probably doesn't value herself. Brynn dug up some background. Ging—uh, that woman—had an unhappy marriage before her husband died."

Cat scowled. "That doesn't give her the right to ruin mine." She pushed her plate aside. "I suppose everybody in town knows by now."

"Not everyone," MJ hedged for her mother's sake. "It's less obvious with Dad back home. Maybe you should come home, too."

"And do what? Get on my knees and beg? I have my pride left, if not much else."

MJ reached across the table and grasped her mother's fingers that had been nervously shredding a paper napkin. "You have me, Mom."

Her mother's eyes teared and she squeezed MJ's fingers. "Yes, thank God, for my beautiful daughter."

But MJ knew, even though her mother loved her deeply, that no one could fill the void her father had created in her mother's world.

MJ had experienced that kind of emptiness when she'd left for New York. She'd had her parents and Nana to love her, but without Grant, something vital had been missing from her life. But she and Grant had only had a short time together. She could only imagine what her mother was feeling at the probability of losing the man who'd been both husband and best friend for over thirty years.

"I've been doing research on the Internet," MJ said, "on infatuation."

Her mother blinked in surprise. "Find anything?"

MJ nodded. "It's amazing the number of scientific studies on the subject."

"Mmm." Her mother's eyes had a vacant look as if she were a thousand miles away.

"Infatuation causes a chemical change in the brain," MJ said. "If Dad's infatuated with…that woman…it explains his change in behavior."

"Infatuation," her mother said with a twist of her attractive lips. "It's the same as love, isn't it?"

"No, that's the good part."

Cat stared across the table at her daughter, giving MJ her full attention. "I could use some good news."

Encouraged, MJ continued. "According to the studies, most infatuations last from eighteen to thirty-six months. And most don't evolve into real love. There has to be more than sexual chemistry involved for love to develop."

"Such as?"

"Things in common. Goals, backgrounds, interests."

"So, according to your research, this infatuation may have your father in its grip for three years." Her mother's smile was lovely but sad. "Now tell me the good news."

"Don't you see, Mom? Dad doesn't have anything in common with…her. Once the infatuation burns itself out, he'll recognize that."

Cat appeared lost in thought. "But a year and a half to three years? A man can make a real fool of himself in that time." She seemed to shake off the idea to concentrate on her daughter. "Your research must have taught you something about yourself."

"Me?" MJ shook her head. "I'm not infatuated with anyone."

This time her mother's expression was warm. "No, you and Grant passed that stage long ago."

MJ didn't want to admit to herself, much less her

mom, how much she still cared about Grant. "I broke our engagement, remember?"

"And I've never really understood why. You two have so much in common—"

"But we fought—"

"Not often." Cat searched her daughter's face and MJ had to look away, afraid of what her eyes might reveal. Cat added, "And you wouldn't have been human if you hadn't."

"But you and Daddy *never* fought."

Cat laughed, looking for a moment almost like her old self. "We never fought in front of you, but we had our differences. And we aired them frequently and with great gusto."

"I don't believe it. I can't remember you two ever not getting along."

"We always did…eventually." Her mother's face softened, as if the memories warmed her. "Although your father and I are both people of very firm opinions, our disagreements were never bitter. We learned to compromise."

The lines of Cat's face hardened again as the pain returned to her eyes. "If you love Grant, sweetheart, let him know. Life's too short to miss out on love."

MJ gasped in disbelief. "How can you say that when Daddy's breaking your heart?"

"Because, in spite of the heartache, I wouldn't trade

anything in the world for the years we've had together. Not even *that woman* can steal the joy of them from me. I'll always have my memories."

Aware of the tears prickling beneath her eyelids, MJ refused to let her mother see them. Cat had enough to worry about without worrying about her, too.

"Promise me you'll think about what I've said," her mother asked.

"Promise," MJ agreed.

But she was careful not to say how much consideration she'd give to loving Grant. She never, ever, wanted to find herself in as much pain as her mother was suffering now.

FOLLOWING THROUGH ON HIS intention to give Merrilee all the space she needed, Grant had been patient. Although the effort had exhausted every ounce of his self-control, he'd left her on her own for a week before contacting her again, hoping she'd get in touch with him instead. When she hadn't, he grabbed the first excuse to seek out her company and telephoned her.

"Come for a ride with me," he begged when she answered.

"Where?" Her voice was unmistakably skeptical.

He didn't want to give away his surprise. "Georgia."

Her laughter floated through the line. "Could you be more specific?"

"Northeast Georgia."

She laughed again, and the familiar bubbly sound warmed him to his toes. "Well, that narrows it down. And why are we going?"

"An errand of mercy."

"A sick animal?"

"Nope."

She paused before saying, "I really should stay here and—"

"Merrilee, it's a surprise. Don't make me spoil it. Just say you'll come."

She'd finally consented to accompany him, but so grudgingly he was beginning to wonder if his certainty that she loved him was merely wishful thinking.

After picking her up at her parents' house, he drove south to the interstate.

"Sorry if I sounded weird when you first called," Merrilee said.

"Not weird, just hesitant." And he thought he understood her reluctance, until her explanation surprised him.

"I've been getting some strange calls lately," she explained.

"Strange?"

"Lots of hang-ups and a couple that were threatening."

Grant felt a chill. "What kind of threats?"

"'Go back to New York where you belong.' That kind of thing."

"All from the same person?"

Merrilee nodded. "A raspy, genderless voice I can't recognize, as if it's being altered electronically for disguise."

"Have you told the police?"

She shook her head.

"Why not?"

He was alarmed for her safety. Even in a sleepy town like Pleasant Valley, bad things happened, and he sure as hell didn't want them happening to Merrilee.

She sighed with what sounded like exasperation. "Because I have a sneaking suspicion the calls might be from Ginger, and I'd rather keep the sordid details of my parents' breakup off the police records."

"Caller ID said it was Ginger?"

"The number's blocked," she said, "but who else would care whether I'm in town or not?"

Merrilee had a point, but Grant couldn't help worrying. "Promise me you'll report it if you get another call."

"What good would reporting it do?"

"The phone company could put a trace on your line and identify the culprit." He shot her a glance, but saw only the back of her head as she stared out the passenger window. "You said the calls were threats, not warnings. What kind of threats?"

"The voice just said I'd be sorry if I didn't leave," Merrilee explained. "If it's not Ginger, it's probably kids playing jokes."

She didn't sound concerned, but Grant's heart was pounding. Ginger could be making the calls out of spite or kids could be jerking Merrilee around, but he didn't want to take any chances.

"If you won't promise to report further threats, I'm calling Brynn myself," he insisted.

He caught her smile then, bittersweet and incredibly lovely. He could tell she thought he was overreacting, and maybe he was, but he'd rather make a fool of himself than risk any harm to her.

"I promise," she said. "Now, how much farther do we have to go?"

"We're close."

He exited I-85 a few miles across the Georgia state line and pulled into a parking space at the first rest area.

One of the prettier spots along the highway, the rest stop looked like a park with its wide green lawns dotted with mature trees. Borders of tulips and daffodils lined the walkways, the first blush of new growth tinged the tree canopy a soft green and a scattering of pink dogwoods added a splash of color. A monument of native stone near the buildings that housed rest rooms sported a bronze plaque memorializing men from the state who'd lost their lives in war.

In the early afternoon of a spring day in the middle of the work week, only a few cars had stopped and less than half a dozen tractor-trailer rigs spotted the truck lot on the opposite side of the parklike lawn from the car parking area.

"We're here," Grant announced and turned off the ignition.

"This is it?" Merrilee gazed around her. "*Now* are you going to tell me why?"

Grant shook his head. "Only that we're waiting for someone."

She cocked her head at an adorable angle and considered him. "You're running drugs and you're waiting for your supplier?"

The humor in her voice pleased him. As long as she could make jokes, she wasn't allowing her parents' breakup to completely dishearten her.

"There's more money in drugs," he admitted, "than what we're here for. In fact, there's *no* money in what we're here for."

"How did I let you talk me into this?" She shook her head in disbelief.

"As I recall, you seemed more than ready to get out of the house."

"You're right. I had cabin fever. I've worked until I'm cross-eyed on query letters with sample photos and chapters for my book. Now that they're mailed to prospective agents, I would have jumped at any excuse for some fresh air."

"Any excuse? Good thing I'm immune to flattery."

Her blush of embarrassment delighted him. "I didn't mean that the way it sounded."

"No offense taken. I didn't know you were working on your book. I thought you were making rounds with your father."

"Only once, day before yesterday. I went with him to treat Mr. Mauney's sow who's off her feed."

"Get any pictures?" Grant opened his door, jumped out and motioned Gloria outside.

Merrilee joined them and fell into step with Grant as he sauntered toward the dog walk. Gloria bounded ahead, chasing a flying insect, her long legs flashing, her gray fur blowing in the breeze.

"I took some great shots of the farm and Mr. Mauney with his pigs," Merrilee said, "but I can't use the ones of Dad."

"You're good, but you can't expect every photograph to be perfect."

"The problem wasn't technique." Sadness filled her voice. "It's the way Dad looked, tired and drawn, as if he's wound tight as a spring and ready to break. I don't want to immortalize that appearance in a book."

"You making any headway in getting him away from Ginger?"

Her feathery brows drew into a frown. "He did mention Mom for the first time after we left the farm that day."

"That's good, isn't it?"

Merrilee shrugged and shoved her hands into the pockets of her jacket as they followed Gloria across the lush grass of the dog walk.

"When we returned home from Mauney's, Dad went into the kitchen to make coffee. Mom had left one of her sweaters folded across the back of a chair in the family room. He picked it up and held it to his face. He must have caught a whiff of her perfume, because his eyes widened and his expression changed, like a man coming out of a deep trance."

Grant took her elbow and steered her toward a bench nearer the parking area. "Too cold? We can wait in the truck."

Her cheeks were deep rose where the chilly breeze had nipped them, but she shook her head. "It's wonderful being outdoors."

She settled onto the bench. Grant sat beside her and Gloria loped toward them and lay at their feet with her head on her paws, listening as if she understood every word, every nuance.

"For that moment, holding Mom's sweater," Merrilee continued, "Dad seemed his old self. He asked, 'How's your mother?'"

Seemingly lost in thought, Merrilee grew quiet. A frown puckered her brow.

"What did you tell him?" Grant prodded.

A sigh of exasperation exploded from her. "I didn't know what to say, didn't know what Mom would *want* me to say. And I was so afraid of saying the wrong thing, I just looked at him."

"That must have been tough."

She nodded. "He left the room, but he took Mom's sweater with him. Whether there's any significance to his action, I haven't a clue."

She looked so forlorn, Grant wanted to slip his arm around her and draw her against him, but he was saved from that impulse by the arrival of the dark green Ford Explorer he'd been expecting.

"He's here." Excitement tinged his words and glittered in his eyes. He pushed hurriedly to his feet and grabbed her hand. "Come on."

"*Who's* here?"

Unable to restrain himself, with a self-satisfied grin, Grant lifted her off her feet and twirled her around before setting her down again.

"It's Jim Dandy to the rescue," he said. "Come meet him."

Chapter Nine

"Jim Dandy?" MJ said breathlessly, trying to keep up with Grant's long-legged stride as he hurried toward the SUV. "That's the name of an old song my parents used to dance to."

Grant glanced at her. With excitement lighting his eyes and coloring the strong angles of his tanned cheeks, his gleeful anticipation reminded her of the boy he'd once been.

"Jim Dandy's also the name of something else." His delightful grin widened. "You'll see."

Her heart gave a hitch at the sight of him, handsome and elated, and she wondered if she should have stayed home, bored but safe from the pull of his contagious enthusiasm.

Instinctively she held back, but he tugged her toward a dark green SUV with West Virginia plates that had pulled into the parking space next to Grant's truck. A short, plump woman with pleasant features and a smile to match Grant's jumped from the driver's side and walked toward them.

"I thought Jim Dandy was a he," Merrilee murmured in a low voice so the woman couldn't hear.

"He is," Grant said.

"Then where is he?"

"Waiting to make an entrance."

"Dr. Nathan?" the woman called.

"That's me." Grant reached the newcomer and shook her hand. "You must be Jean Tabor. And this is Merrilee Stratton."

"Hi," Merrilee said.

She couldn't help smiling at the middle-aged woman. Jean's bright red curls escaped from beneath a pink watch cap in a clash of colors, freckles peppered her flushed complexion and her bright hazel eyes danced with merriment.

"How was your trip?" Grant asked.

"Good weather and clear roads all the way," Jean answered.

"And Jim Dandy?" Grant said.

MJ strained to catch sight of whoever was waiting in the SUV, but tinted windows blocked her view.

"He loves to travel," Jean said. "Ready to meet him?"

"Absolutely." Grant threw MJ a wait-till-you-see-this look and followed Jean to the rear of her car.

Jean lifted the hatch and removed an animal crate not much larger than a shoe box.

"Jim Dandy's in there?" MJ hoped it wasn't a cat. She'd always found felines reserved, standoffish. Give her a big, slobbery dog any day.

Speaking of which, Gloria had followed them and was sniffing the crate. Jean, apparently unintimidated by the dog's huge size, petted Gloria and grinned at Grant. "Looks like you're going from one extreme to the other."

He shot Merrilee a glance. "You'll have to get a picture of Jim Dandy and Gloria together. That'll be quite a shot, a study in contrasts."

"Is he a cat?" MJ asked.

Jean snorted with a look that said she wouldn't be caught dead with such an animal and passed the crate to Grant. "See for yourself. He's probably ready for a good piddle, so you should let him out."

Grant set the crate on the grass by the car, swung open the door and waited.

MJ watched in delight as a tiny chihuahua the color of maple syrup and dressed in a red sweater stepped daintily from the crate, blinked oversize bulging eyes in the brilliant sunshine and stretched.

"Jean's with Chihuahua Rescue," Grant explained, "and makes special deliveries. And that's Jim Dandy."

MJ waited until Jim Dandy relieved himself beneath a nearby boxwood, then scooped the dog into her arms. He snuggled against her contentedly.

"You brought him all the way from West Virginia?" MJ asked.

"Sure did," Jean said with her engaging grin. "The last leg of his trip."

"Where did he start?" MJ said.

"North Dakota," Jean explained.

"Wow," MJ murmured to the little fellow, "you've had quite a journey."

"Someone lost or abandoned him in a bus station in Minot," Jean said. "When no owner came forward, Chihuahua Rescue claimed him. I'm the fourth and final driver in the relay to bring him here."

MJ scratched the tiny animal beneath its chin. Jim Dandy gazed at her with perfect trust in his big brown eyes. "Who could abandon such a sweetheart?"

Jean made a face. "Not everyone loves animals. Or knows how to treat them. That's why we were so glad when Dr. Nathan contacted us via our Web site, asking if we had a dog ready for adoption."

In awe of his thoughtfulness, MJ looked at Grant. "He's for Mrs. Weatherstone, isn't he?"

Grant nodded, seeming pleased with himself. He reached over and petted Jim Dandy. The dog licked his hand and MJ regretted leaving her camera in the truck.

She had to hold back from throwing her arms around

Grant's neck. The more she tried to convince herself that their relationship would never work, the more he proved how lovable he was.

Hold on, she warned herself.

Just because he was considerate of an elderly widow didn't guarantee marital happiness.

"Gotta go." Jean checked her watch. "If I leave now, I'll be home by dark. If I hurry I can miss the storm that's in the forecast."

She reached into her truck again, slid out a box and handed it to Grant. "His food, leash, bedding and medical records."

Grant tucked the box under his arm. "Thanks for your help."

Jean slammed the hatch. "No problem." She reached over and caressed Jim Dandy's head. Her hazel eyes filled with tears. "Goodbye, little guy." She looked at MJ. "I swore I wouldn't get attached to him, but I couldn't help it."

"Mrs. Weatherstone will give him all the care and love he deserves," MJ assured her.

"You need any more chihuahuas adopted, Dr. Nathan, you just give us a call." With a final sniff, Jean climbed into her SUV and drove away.

"Want to go with me to Mrs. Weatherstone's?" Grant asked.

MJ cuddled Jim Dandy. "I wouldn't miss it for the world."

HOURS LATER MJ sat in the waiting room of the clinic, waiting for Grant to examine an ailing cat before he drove her home. She'd been hoping to track down her father, but, according to Fran, Jim was making a house call. Either her dad was the busiest vet on the planet, or he was purposely avoiding her.

So much for Nana's grand scheme, MJ thought with a sigh.

But if she wasn't having much influence on her father, at least she was expanding her portfolio. She was glad she'd remembered her camera this afternoon, because the pictures she'd snapped earlier of Grant presenting Jim Dandy to Mrs. Weatherstone were classics. Anyone viewing them would have to be made of stone if they didn't feel a pull on their heartstrings at the joy on the elderly widow's face, the happiness of the little chihuahua and the kindness that had shone in Grant's smile.

With a mental shake, MJ reminded herself that she absolutely, positively, had to avoid Grant in the future. The more time she spent with him, the harder returning to New York would be.

When they'd left the rest stop, she'd wished Grant had allowed her to hold Jim Dandy on her lap. She'd needed the distraction from Grant, but he'd insisted, and rightly so, that the dog should remain in his crate in the rear seat next to Gloria.

"If we have an accident and the airbag deploys," Grant explained, "the impact could kill the little guy. That's why Gloria always rides in the back."

He'd reached into the back seat and caressed Gloria's long muzzle. Gloria licked his hand and her wagging tail thudded happily against the tiny dog carrier, waking the chihuahua, who barked in high-pitched protest. Grant was obviously the wolfhound's hero and everything in Grant's manner, from the calming touch of his hand to the unspoken love in his eyes, spoke volumes about how much he adored his dog.

MJ turned away, remembering too clearly a time when Grant had looked adoringly at her, making her feel on top of the world with just a glance.

Adoring glances aren't enough to hold a relationship together, she reminded herself.

And she refused to admit how much she missed them.

Once on the interstate, Grant tuned to a soft rock station and the sentimental love ballad filling the cab accentuated MJ's awareness of the man beside her. Her nerve endings hummed at his nearness and the power of his personality pressed on her like the force of gravity. Her chest tightened, making it hard to breathe, but she assured herself the difficulty was caused by warm air pumping from the truck's heater, not Grant's intoxicating proximity. But as much as she tried to keep her eyes on the road ahead, her gaze kept returning to him.

She couldn't deny he was handsome, though not in a hunky movie star way. His hair was too shaggy, a few weeks past needing a trim, and a web of fine lines radiated from the corners of his eyes, the result of too much squinting in the sun. Or too many smiles. His broad shoulders filled out his denim jacket in a way that sent her pulse pounding, and he was incredibly, sexily tall, his head almost brushing the roof of the cab. And, she noted with a repressed grin, he must have dressed hurriedly this morning, because she'd glimpsed two different colored socks when he'd climbed into the truck.

And those magical hands.

His strong fingers gripped the steering wheel, tapping occasionally in time with the music and, in spite of her best efforts, she couldn't stop thinking of the way those hands had touched her in places that had driven her wild. She tamped down the ache those memories evoked.

Every now and then he glanced her way with a look that turned her insides to mush and made her knees weak.

But there was so much more to Grant Nathan than good looks and warm smiles. His innate love of animals. His deep concern for people. And his stick-to-it attitude reflected in the strong set of his jaw.

Not to mention his skills as a carpenter, landscaper and decorator, she thought, recalling the intimate comfort of his home.

How could she guard her heart against such a man? In self-defense, she attempted to catalog his faults. He lost his temper when pushed to his limit. He wouldn't mind staying in Pleasant Valley the rest of his life. He… Her mind went blank. If she was going to use his short-comings to resist him, she was flat out of luck.

But look at her dad, she reminded herself. He had almost no faults, either, and he'd broken her mother's heart.

"You're awfully quiet," Grant said.

"I was wondering how a great guy like my dad could go so wrong." She wasn't about to tell Grant she'd been thinking of him.

"Jim's human," Grant said. "We all make mistakes."

"I know."

But what she didn't know was whether her own mistake was loving Grant or leaving him.

MJ was relieved when they arrived in Pleasant Valley at Mrs. Weatherstone's house, a massive three-story Victorian around the corner from Nana's. The impending visit gave her something to focus on besides Grant.

She gazed at the house through the passenger window of Grant's truck. "Mrs. Weatherstone must be at least eighty-five. I can't believe she lives in this huge place all alone."

Grant shrugged. "We tried to convince her to move or hire a companion. She refuses to go to a retirement home and she insists she doesn't want strangers living with her."

"How does she manage?"

"She uses only the first floor so she doesn't have to climb stairs. She pays several teenagers who shop for her, do the housework and mow her lawn. Brynn checks on her once a day when she's on patrol."

MJ had to admit that the house and lawn looked neat and tidy, even though the flower borders weren't as impressive as she remembered from her childhood.

Grant turned to Gloria in the back seat. "You have to stay, girl. Can't have your tail-wagging destroying Mrs. Weatherstone's knickknacks."

Gloria whined.

"I'll leave the window down," Grant assured the dog. "We won't be long."

He climbed out of the truck, opened MJ's door and held Jim Dandy's crate while she hopped out and slung her camera over her shoulder.

"Should we have called?" MJ asked.

Grant shook his head. "Mrs. Weatherstone's always home and always glad for company."

They mounted the steep stairs to the wide porch and Grant rang the bell next to the oversize double doors with stained-glass panels.

For several long moments the house remained silent. Then a clumping sound grew louder and the front door opened. Mrs. Weatherstone, leaning on a metal walker, beamed at them. "Sorry to take so long. I was in the kitchen making tea. Come in and have a cup."

"No tea for us, thanks," Grant said, "but we would like to visit a minute."

Mrs. Weatherstone seemed a bit more frail, but otherwise exactly as MJ remembered. Tiny in stature with birdlike bones, she was fastidiously dressed in a pink twin set with a string of pearls, a wool skirt in a pink-and-lilac plaid and sturdy black brogans. Short wisps of soft white hair framed her face and accented her violet eyes. And when she smiled, she reminded MJ of a saint pictured in a Sunday school pamphlet.

MJ and Grant followed her into the front parlor. Filled with heavy antique furniture, the room was bright with sunlight streaming through the tall south-facing windows. Grant, who'd held Jim Dandy's carrier behind his back, slid it out of sight beside the sofa as they took their seats. The little dog, as if sensing he was a surprise, kept silent.

"I thought you were in New York City, Merrilee June," Mrs. Weatherstone said. "But I don't get out much these days, so I'm always the last person in town to hear any news."

MJ hoped Mrs. Weatherstone hadn't heard about her father and Ginger Parker. "I'm just home for a short visit."

"That's nice," the old woman said with warm sincerity. "I know Sally Mae's pleased." She turned to Grant. "And it's always good to see you, my dear. You Nathan children are my angels."

She turned back to MJ. "I don't know how I'd live without them. Jodie sends my dinner from the café every day, and any time I need something repaired, Grant fixes it for me."

Grant looked uncomfortable at the old woman's praise. "That's what neighbors do."

But MJ knew that Grant was more than a good neighbor. When folks needed him, he went the extra mile, because that's the kind of man he was.

Excellent husband material, her heart insisted. But her head reminded her of the betrayal of her father, the most excellent of husbands, and reinforced the wall she'd thrown around her emotions.

Grant moved to sit beside Mrs. Weatherstone and took her fragile hands in his big ones. "I'm so sorry about Itty-Bitty."

The violet eyes filled with tears. "I do miss her. My lap seems so empty without her. She was my best friend."

Grant nodded. "And you were hers. She had a long and happy life, thanks to you."

Mrs. Weatherstone pulled a lace-edged handkerchief from her pocket and dabbed her eyes. "The house is so quiet without her. Who would have thought such an itty-bitty dog could fill a house this big?"

"She filled it with love," Grant said.

Mrs. Weatherstone nodded. "I never realized how much I talked to her until she was gone. Now there's no one to talk to. I miss her so much."

MJ swallowed against the lump in her throat.

Grant gave Mrs. Weatherstone's hands a gentle squeeze. "I've come to ask you a favor."

Mrs. Weatherstone sniffed and appeared to shake off her sadness. "Ask anything you want, dear. You always do so many favors for me."

"I have a dog that needs a home."

The old woman's violet eyes flew open wide with consternation. "Not Gloria?"

Grant laughed and shook his head. "Good grief, no. She'd be like a bull in a china shop in this house. Gloria has a home for life with me. But this little fellow was abandoned in a bus stop in North Dakota. Would you like to meet him?"

Mrs. Weatherstone looked hesitant.

"You don't have to agree to anything," Grant said gently. "Just have a look."

"Well, if you put it that way…"

Grant reached over the arm of the sofa, picked up the crate and set it on the floor in front of Mrs. Weatherstone. When he opened the door, Jim Dandy, who'd apparently been asleep, stepped out, stretched and looked around.

MJ held her breath.

As if knowing where his future lay, Jim Dandy hopped onto the footstool near Mrs. Weatherstone's seat, then dived directly into her lap, where he curled up as if he'd been sleeping there all his life.

From the look in the old woman's eyes, MJ could tell it was love at first sight.

"He's precious." Mrs. Weatherstone drew in her breath and ran a trembling hand over the warm little body. "I can't believe nobody wants him."

"I know Jim Dandy can't replace Itty-Bitty," Grant said, "but he needs a good home, and Itty-Bitty would want you to have a companion, now that she's gone."

Tears overflowed and ran down Mrs. Weatherstone's face. She fumbled again for her handkerchief.

"Forgive an old lady for crying," Mrs. Weatherstone said, "but I'm sad and happy. I'll be glad to give this sweet little fellow a home."

MJ understood the woman's mixed feelings, and Grant put his arms around the older woman and hugged her. "Jim Dandy has just won the doggie lottery, Mrs. Weatherstone, being adopted by you. He'll have the best life a dog could have."

Grant kissed the old woman's forehead and MJ snapped a picture, preserving the perfection of the moment for all time.

"You take good care of this young man," Mrs.

Weatherstone patted Grant's hand and spoke to MJ as they were leaving. "He's a keeper."

"I'm not…we're not…" MJ had started to explain, but, not wanting to detract from the old woman's happiness, she had simply nodded.

HE'S A KEEPER.

The words echoed in MJ's head, matching the rhythm of her heart as she sat in the waiting room. She stifled them by thinking of her father. So much for till-death-do-us-part. With more than half of all marriages ending in divorce and her own parents headed in that direction, the thought of any man, even Grant, as a keeper was absurd. If life had taught her anything, it was that love inevitably led to heartache.

She'd be better off with a dog, but as Itty-Bitty had so recently and unhappily proved, even beloved dogs weren't forever.

Wondering how much longer she'd have to wait for Grant or her father to appear, MJ glanced at the clock above the reception desk and reached for another magazine.

The waiting room door opened and a client entered along with a swirling gust of frigid air. The wind carried the woman's fragrance, a heavy, cloying scent of musty gardenias and the unmistakable odor of booze.

The owner of the overpowering perfume, a tall, raw-boned woman with coarse features and dyed auburn hair, was dressed in running shoes and skintight exercise leggings that emphasized her bulging thighs. Once inside, she struggled to shut the door against the prevailing wind, then removed her down jacket to reveal an equally tight tank top, cut low to expose maximum cleavage.

MJ caught a glimpse of the woman's heavy makeup and the aggressive thrust of her large breasts before the newcomer turned away. The blatantly seductive sway of her wide hips as she crossed the room to the reception window seemed wasted, since MJ was the only person in the waiting room.

Fran glanced up and stiffened at the woman's approach. The receptionist's usual sunny smile of welcome froze on her lips.

"Is Dr. Stratton here?" the woman asked.

The nasal Northern accent, combined with Fran's chilly reception, alerted MJ to the woman's identity.

The notorious Ginger Parker.

MJ reeled from the surge of white-hot anger that threatened to propel her from her seat to the woman's throat and she fought for self-control. She had always been impulsive and, as much as she longed to scratch the home-wrecker's eyes out, she dared not behave in any way that would further damage her parents' relationship. In an effort to calm herself, she gripped the edge of her chair with both hands and drew in a deep breath.

"Dr. Stratton is out on a call, Mrs. Parker." Fran's tone was as chilly as the wind that had gusted through the door.

"Then I'll just wait in his office." Ginger's voice had a slight slur, as if she'd had too much to drink.

"I can't allow that," Fran said with obvious distaste, "but you can have a seat in the waiting room."

"Don't you know who I am?" the woman demanded with a snarl in her voice.

MJ felt a stab of pity for Fran.

The receptionist closed her eyes for a second, as if attempting to hold her temper. "You're Mrs. Parker. You were in last year with a canary."

"Oh, I'm much more than a client," Ginger said with a smug smile that threatened to crack the top layer of her makeup. She thrust her left hand forward.

MJ strained to see, but the woman's body obscured her view.

"Genuine emerald, two-carat, with yellow diamond baguettes." Ginger's throaty laugh sounded crude. "All I had to do was mention to Jimmy—"

Jimmy! MJ locked her lips against the protest rising in her throat. No one ever called her father Jimmy, not even when he was a boy.

"—that I *love* emeralds, and he had this special ordered."

Ginger fluttered her hand for the jewel to reflect the light, and MJ caught sight of the obscenely large gem, an utterly tasteless ring that her mother wouldn't be caught dead wearing. The piece was as different from her mother's refined engagement diamond as Ginger's coarseness was from Cat's cool elegance.

"So you see, hon," Ginger continued, and Fran winced at the woman's familiarity, "I'm not just any client. I'm Dr. Stratton's fiancée."

MJ could take no more. She shoved to her feet and stormed across the waiting room.

"Haven't you forgotten something?" She spoke between gritted teeth to keep from shouting in the woman's face.

Ginger swung around, swaying slightly on her feet like a punch-drunk boxer. "Who the hell are you?"

"Dr. Stratton is a married man," MJ said. "How can he be engaged?"

Ginger swished her hand, as if brushing away the facts. "His marriage has been over a long time. The divorce will be just a formality."

MJ opened her mouth for a scathing reply, but several things happened at once before she could speak.

The client with the cat left the examining room and crossed the waiting room toward the door. Gloria, tail wagging furiously, trailed the client into the reception area and, true to her love of women, loped straight for Ginger and gently nuzzled her hand.

"Get away from me, you filthy beast!" Ginger screamed.

With the hand that bore the tacky ring, she slapped the affectionate wolfhound hard in the face. The sickening whack of the blow reverberated through the waiting room, concurrent with Gloria's heartrending yelp of pain and fear.

MJ lunged forward, but Gloria was too fast. The client with the cat carrier had opened the door to leave, and the wolfhound bounded past her, almost knocking the cat's owner down in her haste to escape.

MJ raced out the door after her, but Gloria was already out of sight.

Chapter Ten

Grant stepped into chaos in the waiting room. Wearing attire as cheaply voluptuous as ever, Ginger Parker slouched at the reception window, her face blotched with anger beneath its layers of cosmetics. Fran appeared almost in tears. Merrilee was rushing in the front door.

"Who yelped?" He scanned the room. "Is an animal hurt?"

"Gloria," Merrilee answered, out of breath, her eyes flashing fire, her fists clenched. "Mrs. Parker hit her and Gloria took off. I tried to catch her, but she's gone."

Anger blasted through Grant like a force-ten gale. He turned the full power of his fury on Ginger, whose smug expression lacked the slightest hint of remorse. "You struck my dog?"

"She bit me!" Ginger whined and rubbed the back of her hand against her heavy thigh.

"Gloria doesn't bite." Grant's heart sank. He'd spent months gaining Gloria's confidence and teaching her to trust people again. Ginger's cruelty had shattered his efforts and Gloria's too big heart. No wonder the animal had run away.

"She did *not* bite," Fran was insisting. "I saw the whole thing. Gloria was just being her friendly self. Mrs. Parker had no reason to hit her."

At the same time, MJ was shouting at Ginger, "You're a liar. Gloria was only saying hello."

Ginger shrugged with infuriating indifference and examined her hands. Her long crimson nails resembled talons on a raptor, eager for prey.

Grant looked away in disgust and noted the bloodlust in Merrilee's eyes. He had to separate her from Ginger before more blows were struck.

He turned to Fran. "Cancel my other appointments. I'm going after Gloria." He looked to Merrilee. "Come with me?"

She was already tugging on her coat.

Next, he rounded on Ginger, his voice cold with anger and fear for his dog. "If you *ever* strike an animal again, I'll have you arrested for animal cruelty."

"Sheesh." Ginger tossed her dyed hair out of her eyes. "What's the big deal? It's just a dog. And I didn't hit it hard."

Grant started to respond, but, noting Merrilee's barely contained fury, grabbed her elbow instead and steered her out the front door before she could launch an attack. Grant empathized with her. He'd never struck a woman, never intended to, but if anyone deserved her block knocked off, it was Ginger. She dispersed chaos and destruction in the lives of others like Pigpen in the comics spread a perpetual cloud of dirt.

"Take it easy," he warned Merrilee on the porch and attempted to follow his own advice. "Nothing you say or do can change that woman into a decent human being. And she'd be the first to level charges against you if you threaten her. Right now, we have to find Gloria. Did you see which way she headed?"

Merrilee shuddered, drew in a deep breath as if fighting for control, and pointed west.

Grant's heart sank again. Gloria had headed away from town toward the mountains. With her long-legged, regal stride, she could cover miles in minutes. If she left the highway, and he hoped she did so she wasn't hit by a car again, she could roam the forest for weeks without being found. With her fear of humans strongly resurrected by Ginger's cruelty, the wolfhound would avoid all contact with people.

Grant might as well be looking for a needle in a haystack, but he had to try. A domesticated animal, Gloria wasn't trained to fend for herself, and with a spring snowstorm in the forecast, the dog might die of exposure if she wasn't found soon.

"Get in the truck," he ordered Merrilee.

She didn't question, didn't hesitate. By the time he had the engine started, she had her seat belt fastened.

He drove away from the clinic and turned west onto the highway. "Look for tracks or any signs of a path broken through the underbrush."

Grant switched on the emergency flashers and drove slowly, inching along the road. Too absorbed in their search to make conversation, he and Merrilee scanned the shoulders of the highway and the adjoining fields for any signs of Gloria. Every quarter mile or so, he'd stop and they'd both climb out to comb different sides of the road and call Gloria's name.

They spotted no marks of the dog's passage, heard no answering barks to their cries, and their discouragement grew.

Gloria had completely disappeared.

The western mountaintops had been cloaked by clouds from the approaching storm when they'd set out. In less than an hour, darkness had fallen and flurries of snowflakes filled the air. Despite their continuing search, they still had no sign of Gloria.

Grant stopped again and Merrilee passed in front of the headlights to return to the truck after another futile effort at locating the wolfhound. The intense glare of the beams revealed the pallor of her skin, the thin white line around her mouth and her violent shivering, in spite of her heavy jacket.

When she slid onto the passenger seat, Grant wrapped his arms around her and pulled her against him. "You're freezing."

Expecting her to jerk away, he was surprised when she snuggled against him for warmth.

"I'm not nearly so cold as poor Gloria must be. Besides, I have my anger to keep me warm." She tilted her head toward him and even in the darkness of the cab, fury sparked like blue flames in her eyes. "It's a good thing you got me out of there and away from her. I was ready to commit murder."

"Couldn't let you do that," he murmured against her hair, breathing in the scent of honeysuckle that played havoc with his pulse. "A prison cell definitely limits your scope as a photographer."

With her arms tight around his waist, her shivers were subsiding. "I'm warmer now. Shouldn't we keep looking?"

Snow covered the windshield. Grant flipped on the wipers to clear it. The headlights barely penetrated the heavy snowfall that obscured the road.

"We'd better call it quits for tonight," he admitted with reluctance.

"But Gloria—"

"She's smart enough to find a warm burrow until the snow passes," he said for Merrilee's sake, although he doubted that Gloria, in her frantic state, was reacting to anything but fear. He couldn't find the wolfhound until light came and the weather cleared, but tonight Merrilee needed him. He'd witnessed her fury and devastation at meeting Ginger. Merrilee shouldn't be alone to deal with her turmoil of emotions.

"Come home with me," he offered.

This time she jerked away as if he'd slapped her. "I don't think that's a good idea."

Her refusal hurt, more than he wanted to admit. He reminded himself that she was afraid of her feelings for him, terrified of having her heart broken. But her rejection still smarted.

"Then let me take you to your nana's. You shouldn't chance running into your dad now. You're too angry and you might say something you'll regret."

Merrilee let out a breath, lifting a wisp of bangs that had fallen over her eyes. "You're right. I'd tell him in no uncertain terms exactly what I think of that... that..."

"Hussy?"

"Hussy's not strong enough by far, but I'll settle for it for now." She scooted to her side of the truck and fastened her seat belt. "Take me to Nana's, please. She and I have to talk. Dad's situation is much worse than we thought."

Grant turned the truck and headed toward town. Limited visibility slowed his progress to a creep. "Ginger's worse than you thought?"

"That, too, but she was waving a ring in Fran's face, claiming she and Daddy are engaged."

Grant cursed.

"Say that in front of Nana," Merrilee said dryly, "and she'll wash your mouth with soap."

"Gosh darn," he amended.

By the light from the dashboard, he could see Merrilee grin before her expression sobered again. "Nana's plan isn't working. I'm taking some great pictures, but Daddy's avoiding me like the plague. I can't have any influence on him if I can't get near him."

Grant nodded. For weeks his partner had lived in a world of his own, going about his business as if in a trance that blocked out everyone else. Grant wished he could offer Merrilee some crumb of hope, but if Jim was planning to divorce Cat and marry Ginger, Grant felt helpless to intervene.

The worsening weather soon took his thoughts off the Strattons's imminent breakup. The snow was thickening, ice slicks were forming on the road and howling wind rocked the heavy-duty pickup.

"Sorry," he said, "There's no way we're going to make it into town through this storm. We're almost to my house, though. Okay to stop?"

He didn't want to pressure her, but driving further under these conditions was suicidal.

Merrilee hesitated, then peered through the window at the deepening snow. "Okay, but only until the road's been plowed and salted."

"I have supper ready in the Crock-Pot."

"That woman killed my appetite."

"My secret recipe will bring it back to life."

"Secret recipe?"

He could feel Merrilee's gaze, but he didn't dare take his eyes off the treacherous road to look at her. "Black-eyed peas."

"Nothing secret about them," she said.

"Oh, yeah." Grant smacked his lips in anticipation. "I cook them all day with diced ham, pearl onions and a judicious amount of chopped tomatoes, chili peppers and spices."

"Salsa?"

He grinned. "You got it."

"Not your typical Southern fare," she admitted.

"If you had any sense—" he strove to keep his tone light "—you'd marry me for my cooking."

"If I married you for your cooking, I'd end up weighing three hundred pounds."

"We'd work it off."

"I hate exercise."

"Sex burns a lot of calories."

"But I'd be marrying you for your cooking, not for sex." Her tone was teasing, too.

"Then the sex would be the quid pro quo. I cook. You be the sex goddess."

"Sex goddess?" She laughed and the sound warmed

him more than the hot air from the truck's heater. "That'll never work."

"Why not?"

"You know how to cook, but I've never had a single sex goddess lesson."

You don't need lessons. Every hormone in my body adores you just as you are.

He shoved aside memories of their lovemaking. Those recollections, still vivid after so many years, weren't helpful to his resolution to go slow with Merrilee. And if he didn't concentrate on his driving, he'd land the truck in a ditch.

"Do they have a school for sex goddesses?" he asked in feigned surprise.

"Maybe I could take a correspondence course."

He wiggled his eyebrows. "Can I help with your homework?"

She swatted his arm. "In your dreams."

Yeah, she was in his dreams all right. And now she'd be in his house. For the night, from the looks of the storm. Resigned to a cold shower to cool his jets, he turned into his driveway.

The cold shower wasn't necessary. Remembering Gloria, lost in the horrible weather, doused his ardor. And reignited his furor toward Ginger Parker.

Slipping and sliding on the icy walk, Grant and Merrilee hurried toward the house. Inside, they were greeted by the glow of lights, deliciously warm air, and a spicy aroma from the Crock-Pot.

"At least the power's still on." Grant peeled off his outer garments and headed for his phone, a common routine, since he was always on call. A blinking red light on the handset indicated waiting voice mail.

"A message," he told Merrilee. "I hope it's not an emergency, not in this weather."

MJ PEELED OFF HER sodden jacket and hung it over a ladder-backed chair near the fireplace. Grant touched a match to the kindling while he checked his voice mail on his portable phone.

Gloria's empty bed by the hearth reminded MJ of the dog's plight and Ginger's cruelty. For a moment anger threatened to choke her. Ginger obviously didn't have a solitary shred of human kindness. She'd exhibited no remorse for striking a helpless animal or for breaking up a marriage.

It takes two to tango.

Okay, so her dad was also at fault. But after encountering Ginger, MJ instinctively knew that his involvement with the other woman wasn't cold and calculating, unlike the trap Ginger had set for him. Stressed, overworked, exhausted, and with Cat too often away, MJ's dad had fallen into Ginger's clutches unawares.

What he needed was a wake-up call. And Merrilee had to figure out how to put one through to him.

"The message's from Brynn," Grant said. "She's found out more about our resident home-wrecker and wants to fill us in."

MJ felt like a gawker at a train wreck. She really didn't want to know more about Ginger, but she couldn't help herself. "Call Brynn back."

Grant punched in a number and, from his conversation, MJ gathered he was talking with the dispatcher at the police department.

"Brynn's on a call," he said when he broke the connection. "Traffic accident. The dispatcher will have her phone us when she's free."

MJ sank into the deep leather sofa in front of the fire. When Grant sat beside her, draped his arm over her shoulders and snuggled against her, she didn't resist. She welcomed his presence, his reassuring warmth. She needed a friend and she wanted his advice on how to deal with her father's infidelity.

Infidelity?

Insanity was a better term, especially now that she'd actually seen the infamous Ginger. Her father had to be out of his mind.

"I don't know what to do," she said with a sigh.

"Saving your parents' marriage isn't up to you, despite what your grandmother has implied," Grant reminded her softly but without censure. "Their relationship is their responsibility."

MJ placed her finger on the tip of his nose. "Remember your little lecture about objectivity? There has to be some way to help Dad see what kind of woman he's involved with. And what he's doing to Mom."

Grant grasped her finger and moved it to his lips. His touch sent a shiver of delight up her spine. She knew she should withdraw her hand, but now he held it, kissing her palm with tender little nibbles that drove her senses wild, and all she wanted was to feel his lips on hers, his arms around her.

Sitting next to him, feeling his heat seeping through the layers of her clothes, hearing the calming reassurance of his voice, brought home with a vengeance how much she'd missed him. Only the frenetic pace of New York City living had kept her longing for him at bay. Here in the comfy, peaceful setting of his home, with snow blasting against the two-story windows, she had no buffer against her feelings.

When he slid his other arm around her and lifted her onto his lap, she couldn't resist. Didn't want to, even though her brain was screaming that she was setting herself up for more heartbreak.

But how could she think about heartbreak when his lips were tasting hers and the flick of his tongue was igniting bursts of desire that threatened to set her aflame? She threaded her fingers through his shaggy hair, opened her mouth to his and moaned with pleasure.

Somewhere a noise sounded.

For several seconds, she was too lost in Grant's kiss for the sound to register.

When it happened again, she realized the doorbell was ringing.

Grant lifted his head and stared at the door in disbelief. "Who's out in this storm?"

"Has to be a maniac," MJ observed breathlessly. "And I didn't hear a car."

She didn't add that an eighteen-wheeler could have roared through the room and, lost in the power of Grant's embrace, she wouldn't have noticed.

With a smoldering look that promised he would finish what they'd started, Grant rose from the sofa and went to the door.

Brynn Sawyer blew in with a flurry of snowflakes, her high-energy personality charging the room like an electrical current. "Saw your lights on. I just finished working an accident down the road."

"Anyone hurt?" Grant asked.

Brynn removed her uniform hat, dusted off the snow, and shook her head. "Car slid off the road into a ditch. They're being towed back to town as we speak."

"What are you doing here?" MJ joined them at the door.

"I tried phoning you at the clinic and Fran said you were with Grant. When I spotted his truck and saw the lights on, I took a chance you'd be here."

MJ resisted the impulse to finger-comb her disheveled hair.

"Hope I didn't interrupt anything." Brynn's saucy grin contradicted her words.

"We just got in," MJ said. "We've been searching for Gloria."

"Gloria?" Brynn looked to Grant. "What happened?"

Grant related the wolfhound's run-in with Ginger, and Brynn's face darkened, anger turning her midnight-blue eyes almost black. "When I check in with dispatch, I'll have a bulletin issued for the other officers to be on the lookout for her."

"Thanks," Grant said grimly, "but I'm afraid, even if they come across her, she'll run the other way."

MJ's heart went out to him. Grant loved all animals, but he'd formed a special bond with the wolfhound.

"I was about to dish up supper," Grant said to Brynn. "You hungry?"

"That fabulous smell would make anyone hungry," Brynn said. "It's time for my supper break, but I can't make it back to town until the plow comes through."

"Then eat here," Grant offered. "You can tell us the latest on Ginger Parker over supper."

"Deal. But I can't promise what I say won't spoil your appetite." Brynn stripped off her heavy jacket and gloves, keyed the mike on her radio and checked in with dispatch.

MJ went to the kitchen, took out place mats and silverware, and set the table. Grant began assembling a salad, just as he'd done the other evening. They were working together, each at his own task, like a long-married couple.

Brynn finished her call and joined them in the kitchen. "Need help?"

"It's under control," Grant said.

"No, thanks." MJ added. "From the sound of the storm, you have a long night ahead. You'd better relax while you can."

Brynn's grin widened. "I see you know your way around the place, Merrilee."

"What's that supposed to mean?" MJ shot a look at Grant, but could see only the back of his head and the broad expanse of his shoulders as he spooned food from the Crock-Pot.

"Come here often?" Brynn was goading her, but MJ refused to rise to the bait.

Grant saved MJ from answering by handing each of them a full plate before he turned to the microwave, where he'd heated cornbread from the freezer. MJ and Brynn took their seats and Grant joined them at the table.

"Looks good enough to eat," Brynn joked.

Grant passed her cornbread. "This'll have to do. I'm fresh out of doughnuts."

"Funny man." Brynn took a bite of food and jerked her head toward MJ. "You should have married him while you had the chance. Now that I know he can cook like this, I may snap him up myself."

If MJ hadn't known her friend was teasing, she might have worried. As gorgeous as Brynn was, any man she set her sights on was doomed. But Brynn was also a cynic, probably made that way by the criminals she encountered in her work. A man would have to be an icon of perfection to win her jaded heart.

But MJ wasn't interested in marrying Grant, she assured herself, so why worry?

She swallowed a bite of cornbread. "Did you find out anything useful about Ginger?"

"Tons. Her life reads like a Harold Robbins' novel."

"Glamorous?" Grant asked.

Brynn shook her head. "Smutty."

MJ groaned and set down her fork. "I'm not sure I want to hear this."

"You don't have to, if you'd rather not." Brynn dug into her black-eyed peas with gusto.

MJ returned Grant's gaze across the table. His deep brown eyes held sympathy. And a deeper emotion she didn't want to recognize.

"Brynn's right," Grant said. "No need to torture yourself. We all know what kind of woman she is."

Steeling herself for the worst, MJ took a deep breath. "Tell me everything, Brynn. I'm desperate to free Daddy from that awful woman's clutches."

"She'll eventually drop him like a hot potato," Brynn said.

MJ blinked in surprise. "How can you be sure?"

"That's her modus operandi. And that's also why she left New Jersey and changed her name."

Grant leaned forward, his curiosity obviously piqued. "She was running away from a man?"

"Make that men, plural," Brynn said.

Her friend must have noted the puzzlement MJ felt, because she added, "I'd better start at the beginning."

"Good idea," Grant said.

MJ felt her stomach tighten. Whatever Brynn was about to say wasn't good, but MJ had to hear it. She owed it to her parents to arm herself with any facts that might help save their marriage.

"I've already told Merrilee about Ginger's domestic disputes with her late husband," Brynn said to Grant. "Now I've found out what our resident tramp was up to from the time her husband died until her arrival in Pleasant Valley."

"New Jersey madam?" Grant suggested.

"You're close," Brynn said. "She was apparently the queen of cybersex."

MJ gawked at Brynn. "What does that mean?"

Brynn laughed. "For all your time in the big city, Merrilee, you're such an innocent." Her laughter faded. "Cybersex means Internet chat rooms where people exchange sexually explicit messages. Ginger was active online, particularly in chat rooms for married people looking for some extracurricular excitement."

"How do you know all this?" Grant said. "I didn't think you could access someone's computer files without a warrant."

"I'm coming to that part," Brynn said. "Be patient. It's a long and sordid story."

MJ closed her eyes. "Let's get it over with."

"According to my contact at the local New Jersey police department, Ginger filed stalking complaints against several men. When the P.D. investigated, they discovered that the men whom Ginger had claimed were stalking her were rejected lovers, guys she had met in the chat rooms. She'd had an online affair with each of them, exchanging sex chat that eventually evolved into phone sex and actual in-person rendezvous."

MJ shuddered with revulsion.

"If she was giving them what they wanted," Grant said, "why were they stalking her?"

"They weren't, actually," Brynn explained. "Once Ginger tired of them or they insisted on marrying her, filing charges was her way of getting rid of them."

MJ shook her head, confused. "Why get rid of them if their attention's what she wanted?"

Brynn scowled. "Seems Ginger was anxious only for the thrill of the chase and the booty it provided. These men had given her expensive gifts, taken her on luxurious trips and asked her to marry them."

"Whoa." Grant tipped back in his chair and scratched his head. "Am I missing something? You said she met these guys in chat rooms for married people. If they're married already, how could they marry her?"

"After they divorce their wives." Brynn scowled. "That's the really crazy part. Ginger Parker is one sick puppy. She apparently loves the chase, the power and control of leading men on, breaking up their marriages, then leaving them in her dust."

Bile rose in MJ's throat and she swallowed hard against it. "What kind of monster is she?"

"A very twisted one." Brynn, who didn't have a dog in this particular hunt, hadn't lost her appetite. She was polishing off the last of the peas with a piece of cornbread. "I checked with the psychiatrist our department contracts with. According to him, women like Ginger are addicted to married men because they fear genuine emotional involvement. With a married man, the relationship is always tentative, somewhere off in the future, based on what's going to happen down the road, once the guy gets his divorce—"

"Once he's over the rebound from his wife." A light had gone on when MJ recalled Ginger asking her dad to move out.

Grant shook his head. "Why doesn't Ginger just avoid men if she doesn't want a relationship?"

"That would spoil her fun," Brynn explained. "The shrink says Ginger actually hates men. Her goal is to punish them for something that's happened in her past—"

"Her husband's abuse?" MJ asked.

"According to the shrink, it's more likely something in her childhood," Brynn said. "Like being abandoned by her father or physically or sexually abused by a male relative."

MJ shuddered and Grant reached across the table and grasped her hand. She found herself hanging on to him like a lifeline, soaking up his warmth to ward off the cold that gripped her.

"So what we have is a good-news, bad-news scenario," Grant said.

Brynn nodded. "The good news is, once Ginger's milked Merrilee's dad for all the gifts and excitement she can, she'll move on to her next victim. Actually, she probably already has several suckers dangling online, ready and waiting."

MJ struggled to speak past the anger that constricted her throat. "The bad news is, by the time Ginger drops him, my parents' marriage may be damaged beyond repair."

Chapter Eleven

Grant cleared the table and poured coffee, his concern growing for Merrilee, who'd turned paler with each of Brynn's revelations. Hell on earth, he decided, was watching someone you loved suffer and not being able to do a damned thing about it.

Just as Merrilee was unable to rescue her folks, Grant felt powerless to ease her pain. And the worse her parents' situation grew, the more his hopes of overcoming her fears of loving him dwindled. Witnessing her mother's devastation had only intensified Merrilee's determination to guard her own heart.

But he couldn't simply stand by and do nothing. Every problem had a solution if you searched hard enough for it. Grant had to find a way to bring his usually reasonable partner to his senses. And back to his wife.

Grant handed Brynn cream for her coffee. "Why

don't you write up what you've learned? Merrilee could show her dad the facts and spoil Ginger's fun."

"Nothing's official," Brynn said quickly, "except the stalking complaints Ginger filed. Everything else from my source was off the record."

Merrilee's expression had brightened momentarily, but quickly dimmed. "Showing Dad the complaints could boomerang. He might feel sympathy for Ginger being hounded by those awful men. I can hear her now, rationalizing her behavior, just as she did hitting Gloria."

"Your dad's living in a fantasy." Grant longed for an instant cure to erase the pain in Merrilee's eyes. "How do we bring him back to reality?"

"Reality," Brynn suggested, "would be Jim, Cat and Ginger in the same room. Hard for him to avoid facing facts under those circumstances."

"I can't get Mom home from Asheville," Merrilee said with obvious frustration, "much less in the same room with Dad. Even *I* can't stay in the same room with him long before he's off again."

His friend and partner's marriage was crumbling before his eyes. And that disaster was strengthening every fear Merrilee had of commitment. Determined to solve both problems, Grant cast about for answers. His glance fell on the calendar hanging next to the refrigerator.

"I have an idea," he announced.

"Nothing against the law," Brynn warned in a facetious tone. "If it is, you'd better wait till I leave to discuss it."

"What do you have in mind?" The hope flaring in Merrilee's eyes almost undid him.

"A party," he said.

"A party?" Merrilee asked, and Brynn looked dubious.

"A small, intimate dinner party." Grant counted off the names on his fingers. "Merrilee, me, Jim and Cat, your nana…and Ginger."

"Whew!" Brynn shook her head. "That's a lethal combination. How do you plan to pull it off?"

"I'll have the party here." He turned his gaze to Merrilee. "To celebrate your birthday next week."

Merrilee flushed with apparent pleasure. "You remembered."

"I've never forgotten," he said softly.

From the corner of his eye, he caught Brynn looking from Merrilee to him and grinning like a cat that had fallen into a puddle of cream.

Merrilee set her coffee cup on its saucer with a clatter and frowned. "It'll never work."

"Why not?" Brynn asked.

"Ginger won't come if she knows Mom and Nana will be here," Merrilee said.

"Then we won't tell her," Grant said. "As far as Jim

and Ginger are concerned, it will be just the four of us. And not even Jim can refuse an invitation from his partner to his own daughter's birthday party."

"That's lying," Merrilee protested.

Grant nodded. "Desperate times, desperate measures. If we tell your nana and mother the plan, do you think they'll come?"

Before Merrilee could respond, Brynn's radio crackled to life.

"Snowplow's cleared the highway from town to the west end of the valley," the dispatcher's voice sounded in the room.

"Ten-four," Brynn responded and pushed back from the table. "I'll leave you to plot while I get back to work. With all this ice and snow, it's going to be a busy night."

Grant stood, too. "Before you go, there's something I'd like you to check into."

As if sensing what he was about to ask, Merrilee's eyes widened in alarm. "I told you I didn't want…"

Grant cut her off. "Brynn will keep things confidential. And I need to make sure you're safe."

Brynn tensed, suddenly on full alert. "Safe? What's up?"

"Nothing," Merrilee said with a firmness that defied contradiction.

Brynn looked from Merrilee to Grant. "Help me out here, folks. Is there a problem or not?"

"You going to tell her?" Grant asked Merrilee. "Or should I?"

"There's nothing to tell," Merrilee insisted.

"You've inherited your father's stubborn streak," Grant said gently.

Brynn was watching them both closely and Grant could almost see the gears turning behind her eyes. She placed her hands on her hips and raised her eyebrows in a searing look that had to serve her well when grilling suspects. "This have anything to do with somebody letting the air out of your tires last week, Merrilee?"

Grant had to give Brynn credit. The police officer's mind operated like a computer, making connections at lightning speed. He glanced at Merrilee. "Well?"

"Oh, all right," she conceded and turned to Brynn. "Grant's making a mountain out of a molehill. He wants me to tell you about threatening calls I've had."

"I'm listening," Brynn said.

Merrilee told Brynn what she'd shared with Grant earlier about the telephone threats. "I'm guessing it's either Ginger trying to get rid of me or kids with too much time on their hands."

"Kids?" Brynn looked thoughtful, and Grant wondered if she had a suspect in mind. "Could be. I'll check around. Let me know if the calls continue." She donned coat, hat and gloves. "Thanks for supper, Grant. And good luck with your dinner party."

"Be careful out there," Merrilee said.

"See ya later." Brynn touched her fingers to her cap in a salute. Mischief glinted in her eyes. "Y'all stay warm."

Grant watched until Brynn climbed into her SUV and drove off into the swirling snow, then he shut the door and returned to the living room. Merrilee had curled into the recliner by the fire, her expression unreadable but exhaustion evident in the weary slump of her shoulders. Fighting off his own fatigue, he sank into the rocker opposite her, too tired to speak. Gloria's empty bed reproached him and he vowed to resume his search at dawn, whether the storm had passed or not.

"You're worried about Gloria, aren't you?" The understanding in Merrilee's voice soothed him.

"And you, too," he added.

"The phone threats?"

He nodded. "And the way you're beating yourself up over your parents' problems."

Merrilee sighed and the desolation in the sound went through him like a knife. "I can't believe Daddy's fallen for such a horrible woman."

"Ginger's a master of deceit, according to Brynn. And she's had plenty of practice manipulating men. Jim's misfortune was running into someone like her when he was vulnerable."

Merrilee lifted her head. The flickering flames from the fireplace reflected in her eyes and cast a golden glow on her pale cheeks. She'd never looked more beautiful. Or more unhappy. Grant called on all his self-control to keep from sweeping her into his arms and carrying her upstairs to the bed in the loft. As much as he wanted her, now wasn't the time. Racked by frustration, he wondered if he'd ever hold her again and love her as he'd ached to for six long years. Sex with Merrilee had been great, but he wanted more than the physical release of lovemaking. He wanted to cherish her, laugh with her, and spend the rest of his days with her at his side. He had a home, but the heart of it was missing without Merrilee.

His life could be the lyrics of a country-western song. He'd lost his girl and he'd lost his dog. If it didn't hurt so damned much, it would almost be funny.

Merrilee's voice interrupted his introspection. "Do you really think the dinner party idea will work?"

"If your mom and nana will come, it might."

"Nana will see that Mom does," Merrilee said. "But it's risky. If I were Mom, I'd be tempted to scratch Ginger's eyes out. You might be initiating World War III, right in your own living room."

Grant shook his head. "Your mother and grandmother are class acts. When your dad compares your mom to Ginger, he has to recognize his mistake."

"And if he doesn't?" Anxiety upped her voice an octave.

"Then we tried."

Merrilee shivered in spite of her proximity to the blazing fire. "And I can go back to New York."

"Don't." The plea slipped out before he could stop it.

Looking more dejected than he'd ever seen her, she refused to meet his eyes. "I'm here only to help my folks. If I can't do that, I might as well leave."

I need you, he wanted to say, but he clamped his jaw against the words. The time wasn't right. Disheartened, he wondered if the timing would ever be right.

The telephone rang, shattering the silence.

"That might be your dad," Grant said. "He's probably worried whether you're out of this weather."

He rose and picked up the hand set.

"Grant," a familiar male voice said. "I'm glad the phones are working."

Merrilee glanced at him and he shook his head to indicate it wasn't her father.

"Hey, Jeff. What's up?" Grant hoped none of Jeff's animals was sick. He'd have a devil of a time making it up the mountain through the ice and snow.

"Just wanted you to know I found something of yours," the ex-Marine said.

Grant racked his brain. Had he left supplies or equipment at the Davidson place during his visit last week?

"You should plan to pick her up as soon as the storm

clears," Jeff continued. "She's eating me out of house and home."

Relief shot through Grant like a rocket. "You found Gloria!"

Merrilee perked up at his words.

Grant listened to Jeff's explanation, expressed his thanks and replaced the hand set.

"Is Gloria okay?" Merrilee asked.

Grant nodded. "Jeff found her huddled on the leeward side of his barn when he went out to check on his animals during the storm."

"She didn't run away from him?"

"That's the amazing part," Grant said. "Jeff called her and she came right to him. Followed him inside and ate most of the meat loaf he'd made for his supper."

Merrilee's beaming smile was a welcome sight. "Jeff made friends with her when we were there last week. Gloria must have remembered him."

"I'll pick her up tomorrow if the road's passable."

With the gracefulness of a dancer, Merrilee rose from the chair and crossed the room. "Speaking of roads, the dispatcher told Brynn the highway's clear all the way to town."

He'd wanted her to spend the night. If not in his bed, merely having her under the same roof was consolation enough. He repressed a sigh. "I suppose you want to go to your nana's?"

Merrilee nodded. "I can fill her in on our plans for next week and ask her to recruit Mom into the scheme."

He couldn't fault her logic, but his heart wasn't interested in reason. He reached for her and enfolded her in his arms. Her head fit beneath his chin as if they were matching parts of a puzzle. Contentment flooded him when she didn't pull away but wrapped her arms around his waist and laid her head against his chest.

"Thank you," she murmured against the front of his shirt.

"For dinner? You're welcome."

She shook her head. "For that, but most of all, for being my friend. I need a friend right now more than ever."

"I'll always be your friend, Merrilee." He tipped her face toward him. "The best you ever had. I'm here whenever you need me."

He dipped his head, seeking her lips with his own.

"Please, don't kiss me." Her protest was soft, wavering.

He drew back. "Not if you don't want me to."

Torment shone in her eyes. "That's the problem. I want you to, too much."

With his hand in her hair, he clasped her against his chest, embracing her in a hug. "Don't worry, Merrilee. Everything's going to be all right."

She sighed against his shirt. "You told me that already."

"I did?" He couldn't remember.

"In a dream," she explained.

He held her for a moment longer and optimism built within him. If she dreamed about him and wanted him to kiss her, maybe his chances of overcoming her fears were better than he'd thought.

He gave her a final gentle squeeze and released her. "Get your coat. I'll drive you to Nana's."

He had a spring in his step as they went out the door. He'd found his dog. Now all he had to do was win Merrilee's trust.

"I'LL SEE YOU at Grant's, Daddy."

MJ leaned down to kiss her father's cheek. Reclining in his favorite chair in the family room, he was finishing the newspaper before leaving to pick up Ginger for tonight's party.

"A bit early, aren't you?" her father asked.

MJ's heart pounded and sweat slicked her palms. She'd never been much good at deception. Would her father see through her? She struggled for control and spoke in a voice amazingly calm, considering the turmoil inside her. "I promised Grant I'd give him a hand in the kitchen."

"Okay, princess. See you soon."

She exerted all her efforts to keep from running out the door and down the walk. She slid behind the wheel of Nana's car, started the engine and drove around the block so her dad wouldn't notice she'd headed toward Nana's to pick up her mother and grandmother.

When tonight is over, no matter what the outcome, I'm having a nervous breakdown, she promised herself, only half kidding.

The past few days had been the most nerve-racking of her life, despite signing with an agent who was anxious to represent her proposed book. Her constant second-guessing whether the dinner party would turn out to be a good idea or a disaster had left her no time to worry if her project would sell. At least the agony of indecision over the upcoming confrontation between her parents and Ginger had been a welcome relief from the torment of thinking about Grant.

She couldn't deny that she loved him. Loved him more than her career. More than life itself. The more time she spent with him, the stronger her love grew. And that was the problem. If she succumbed to that love, gave in to the desire to remain in Pleasant Valley and marry him, how would she survive if their marriage didn't meet her high expectations? Or fell apart like her parents'?

Whoever said "better to have loved and lost than never to have loved at all" had to be a fool. Better not to know what she was missing than to experience the ultimate happiness and have it someday suddenly snatched away. Her mother was the living, breathing case in point.

MJ parked the car in front of Nana's. Her mother and grandmother were waiting on the porch and quickly descended the stairs and hurried toward the car.

No one would have guessed from Cat's appearance the heartache she suffered. Her makeup artfully concealed the shadows beneath her eyes and brought a glow of color to her pale cheeks, and yet, in spite of cosmetics, she maintained a natural look. Dressed in tailored, gray wool slacks, a silk blouse in a pale rose and a cardigan that matched her slacks, Cat, although several pounds thinner than her usual weight, was as beautiful as ever.

She opened the back door for Nana, then climbed into the front seat next to her daughter. "I don't know if this is a good idea."

"Fiddlesticks," Nana said. "It can't hurt, and it might help."

"Oh, it can hurt all right," Cat said with a shiver.

MJ couldn't imagine what her mother would feel, seeing her husband with the infamous other woman. "I'll take you home now if you want."

Cat shook her head. "I'm no coward. And maybe Grant's right. Seeing us together as a family again might bring Jim to his senses." A deep sigh escaped her. "And if it doesn't, I'd have to face Jim and Ginger together eventually. Pleasant Valley's my home. I can't stay away forever."

I can't stay away forever.

But that was exactly what MJ intended to do. No matter the outcome of tonight's dinner, she would return to New York tomorrow. Her father was avoiding her too much for her to complete her photographs. Her flight was booked. Her bags were packed. Call her a coward, unlike her mother, but better to leave now with her heart aching but intact.

When they arrived at Grant's, MJ had to admire her mother's poise. Only the slight tremor of her hands belied her outward calm. MJ was a nervous wreck. After dropping a plate that smashed on the tile floor of the kitchen, she was relegated to the living room by Grant while he put the finishing touches on dinner.

Fortunately they didn't have long to wait. Grant answered the door and admitted Jim and Ginger. MJ couldn't decide which of the pair appeared more stunned at the sight of Cat and Nana.

From her bed beside the hearth, Gloria issued a low growl when she saw Ginger and bared her teeth.

"No, girl," Grant ordered quietly. "Stay."

"You didn't tell me *she* was going to be here," Ginger hissed at Jim and glared at Cat. Her grating voice echoed in the tall expanse of the room.

Jim didn't seem to hear her. His gaze fixed on Cat

like a man coming out of a deep coma. When he spoke, his voice was gentle, almost a caress. "Cat. I didn't expect to see you."

Cat rose from her chair and approached the couple. "You didn't think I'd miss our only daughter's birthday celebration?"

MJ didn't know how her mother managed the easy, conversational tone. She was even more surprised when Cat extended her hand to Ginger.

"I'm Cat Stratton. You must be Ginger Parker."

Ginger ignored the outstretched hand. "Soon to be Ginger *Stratton*."

Ginger's words were harsh and they matched the rest of her. Standing face-to-face, the women were a study in contrasts. Cat, the picture of casual, well-bred elegance. Ginger, coarse and vulgar in her too tight, too red, too short dress. With her hair piled high in disarray, diving neckline, black stockings and stiletto heels, she reminded MJ of a hooker.

Her father would have to be blind not to see the striking difference between Ginger and his wife.

"Ginger Stratton," Cat repeated without flinching. "I suppose best wishes are in order."

MJ would have found the look on her father's face comical if she hadn't felt such pain for her mother.

"It's not…we aren't…I don't…" At a loss for words, Jim seemed in danger of whiplash as he snapped his gaze from one woman to the other with the expression of a man caught in the path of an oncoming locomotive.

"Come in and have a drink." Grant gestured toward the living room. "Dinner's almost ready."

"No thanks." Ginger tossed her head in a fit of temper. "We're leaving."

"But, Ginger," Jim pleaded, "it's Merrilee's birthday."

Ginger's face contorted in an ugly scowl. "I don't care if it's the Queen of England's birthday, Jimmy, you'll take me home. Now."

She swiveled on her high heels, stomped out the door and slammed it behind her.

"Well." Nana, in her usual dry tone, spoke for the first time. "That's the first time I've seen trash take itself out."

Jim, dazed and disoriented, approached MJ and grabbed her hands. "I'm sorry, princess. I have to go."

MJ fought back tears. "I'm sorry, too, Daddy."

Before he left, Jim flashed Cat a beseeching look, then fled out the door. Within seconds, the sound of his truck leaving reverberated throughout the room.

Cat wore the frozen look of repressed emotions. "Well, that certainly went well."

MJ felt Grant's arm encircling her shoulders with a consoling squeeze, but she didn't dare look at him, afraid she'd burst into tears if he appeared the least bit sympathetic.

"I think," Nana said with a forceful nod, "that it couldn't have gone better."

"What?" The word exploded from Cat as if she'd been struck. "How can you say that? In case you didn't notice, Jim left with that slut."

"Ah," Nana said, "but he wanted to stay. I saw it in his eyes."

"And Ginger wasn't exactly Miss Congeniality," Grant added. "She showed her true colors. And her nasty disposition."

Nana gave Cat a hug. "We have cause to celebrate, in addition to my granddaughter's twenty-eighth birthday."

Grant dropped his arm from MJ's shoulder and motioned toward the dining table. "Then let's eat."

DINNER DIDN'T TAKE LONG. In spite of the delicious meal Grant had assembled, only he and Nana ate. MJ and her mother took obligatory bites and complimented his cooking, but MJ couldn't swallow anything else past the lump in her throat.

She hadn't known what to expect from tonight's party, but unlike Nana, she didn't believe her father's actions were a good sign.

After ice cream and a chocolate pound cake Jodie

had baked for the occasion, Nana pushed back her chair. "Although it's your birthday, Merrilee June, I'm leaving you to help Grant clean up."

Alone with Grant, on her last night in Pleasant Valley? No way. "I don't have a car—"

"No problem," Grant said quickly. "I'll drive you home."

"Thank you," Nana said with a regal nod. "That will give Cat and me a chance to talk."

"You can drop me off at Dad's," MJ said. "Then you can talk."

"And leave Grant with all this work," Nana said in a scandalized tone, "after all the trouble he's already gone to?"

MJ narrowed her eyes and considered her grandmother, smelling matchmaking like a hound scents coon, but Nana was the picture of innocence. After thanking Grant for his hospitality, she hustled Cat before her out the door. Cat, apparently still shell-shocked by her encounter with Ginger, murmured an almost unintelligible goodbye.

At the click of the front door latch MJ found herself alone with Grant. She hastened to begin clearing the dessert dishes from the table to avoid the heat in his eyes.

Grant took the plates from her hands, placed them in the sink and grasped her by the shoulders. "Leave the rest and come sit with me. We need to talk."

"There's nothing more to say."

Ignoring her protests, he steered her into the living room, then pulled her next to him onto the sofa.

MJ sat rigidly, placing as much distance as possible between them and bracing herself to reveal her plans, which she'd kept from Grant until now. "I'm flying back to New York tomorrow."

Grant grew suddenly still, as if he'd stopped breathing. Silence, except for the ticking of the mantel clock, filled the room. After a long minute he finally spoke. "But your book…"

Why should her book pan out when nothing else had? "A pie-in-the-sky dream. There's no point in finishing it. The whole idea was to reunite my folks. It obviously didn't work."

He cupped her face in the palm of his hand. Despite her best intentions to remain detached, she leaned into his touch.

"Don't give up on dreams, Merrilee. They make life worth living."

"What if dreams turn into nightmares?"

"Are you talking about your parents? I'm talking about us."

"There is no us, Grant."

He placed his other hand on her face and forced her to meet his gaze. The love glowing in the deep molten-brown of his eyes was unmistakable. "Deny it all you want, Merrilee, but you can't change facts. I've never stopped loving you. Look me in the eye and swear you don't love me."

She tried to turn away, but he held her firm. She closed her eyes, but blocking her vision only intensified her awareness of his touch, the warmth of his palms against her cheeks, the chocolate-coffee scent of his breath. Heat surged through her like magma in a long-dormant volcano building toward eruption.

"You can't say it, can you?" he demanded.

"You know I can't."

"Don't leave."

Purposely misunderstanding, she opened her eyes and twisted her mouth in a wry grin. "Since you're my transportation, I can't go until you take me."

Too late, she realized the double meaning of her words.

"Only if you let me."

He waited a millisecond for her to protest before his lips devoured hers and she opened her mouth to him. Shifting his hands from her cheeks to entwine them in her hair, he drew her closer.

Drawing on all her inner resources, she finally wrenched away. "This is pointless. I'm leaving tomorrow, Grant, and I won't be back."

He cupped her face in his hands. "Then let me have tonight, Merrilee. Just one night to remember."

"It's not a good idea," she protested over the yearnings of her heart. Leaving him would be hard enough as it was.

"Then think of it as a goodbye gift," he said softly and lowered his lips to hers.

Reaching deep inside for the will to resist, she came up empty. Every cell in her body longed for him and her nerves sparked like frayed electrical cords. She felt the flick of his tongue against hers and a burgeoning heat flared in her lower body.

Abruptly he drew back, leaving her breathless and wanting more. His lips lifted in a sensuous smile. "I've never shown you the rest of the house."

Oh, lordy. The bedroom was the only part she hadn't seen.

Before she could respond, he swooped her into his arms and started up the stairs.

Stop him now, before it's too late, an inner voice warned her.

But she'd crossed the boundary of reason when he'd kissed her. Now her only reality was the comfort of his embrace, a safe haven against the craziness in her world. She buried her face against his chest, tightened her arms around his neck and beneath her cheek felt the thunder of his heartbeat synchronize with her own. The haven Grant offered was safe, but it was no calm harbor. Her emotions churned, her senses reeled and desire blazed through her like a forest fire out of control.

In the spacious loft Grant set her on her feet and kissed her again while he removed her clothes. Crazy with love, trembling with need, she stripped off his and they fell in a tangle of arms and legs onto the bed.

"Merrilee, I've missed you so much," he murmured, then trailed kisses down her throat. His hands stroked her back and drew her along the length of him, enfolding her in his warmth.

He dipped his head to nuzzle her breasts and slid his fingers between her legs, his expert feathery strokes producing a delicious tension.

"Don't—" she cried.

He raised his head, his eyes questioning.

"Don't stop," she begged. "Please."

He smiled and his magical hands continued until she experienced an explosion of sensation that melted her bones.

Before she could catch her breath, he removed a foil packet from the nightstand, tore it open and slid on the condom. She tilted her hips to meet his plunge, then wrapped her legs around him. He moved with slow, easy strokes, his eyes never leaving hers.

For the first time since she'd returned to Pleasant Valley, she felt she'd truly come home to the place where she belonged. To Grant's arms, his home, his bed. Tomorrow she'd be gone, but she could savor tonight, treasure the moment.

She felt the tension building again and when he slipped over the edge, she followed him in an intense, white-hot burst.

Grant eased his weight off her, pulled her into the crook of his arm and stroked her hair. "I love you, Merrilee."

For the first time in six years, she felt complete, but she couldn't bring herself to say the words. Their lovemaking had been perfection. Tonight had been a birthday present to herself, a moment to treasure in the long, lonely days ahead.

Dreams might shatter, she reminded herself, but memories were forever.

Chapter Twelve

MJ climbed the hated four flights of stairs to her apartment, anxious to strip off her clothes and soak under a hot shower. The seven-year-old's birthday party she'd just photographed had ended in an all-out food fight and cake icing flecked her clothing and glistened in her hair. She'd been lucky to protect her equipment from the sticky barrages. With a grim nod, she decided to add a whopping hazardous-duty fee to the bill for her services.

She'd been back in New York almost three weeks, but in many ways, she felt she'd never left. Except for longing for Grant in the wee hours of the morning when she couldn't sleep. And worrying about her parents. She hadn't spoken with her folks since the disastrous dinner party. Nana had driven her to the airport and promised to report any news, but, ominously, MJ hadn't heard from Nana, either.

The only news she'd had was from her agent. He'd found a publisher interested in her pictorial book on country vets. But, as much as she'd enjoyed returning home and being with family and friends in the place she could no longer deny loving, MJ had no intention of returning to Pleasant Valley to complete her photographs for the project. She couldn't bear watching her father continue to break her mother's heart. And the idea of being around Grant scared her to death. She'd come too close to succumbing to his marriage proposal the night of her birthday. She'd needed all her strength to slip away in the predawn hours to catch her flight.

She entered her apartment and almost dropped her camera bag in alarm. Her parents rose from the sofa and stood with their arms around each other in the early evening light streaming through the tall windows.

"Mom! Dad! What are you doing here?"

Her mother enfolded her in a hug, either not noticing or not caring about the frosting that covered her. "Phil and Randy across the hall had your spare key and let us in."

"Hi, princess." Her father embraced her, too, then held her at arm's length and flicked a piece of icing from her hair. "Rough day?"

Confusion and hope bubbled through her. Her parents were together! But what were they doing here? A chilling thought struck her. "Nana?"

Her mother smiled. "She's fine and sends her love."

MJ stowed her coat and equipment in the closet. "Can I get you something to drink?"

"No thanks," her dad said. "We're taking you to the

best restaurant in New York for dinner. We'll have drinks then to celebrate."

"Celebrate?" MJ asked.

Cat's eyes twinkled. "The demise of Ginger Parker."

MJ's jaw dropped. "She's dead?"

"Not literally," her father said, "but definitely as far as our family's concerned."

"Come sit between us," her mother said.

MJ settled between her parents on the sofa.

"First," Jim said, "I owe you an apology, princess, for my horrible behavior. I hurt you and your mother terribly, and I intend to spend the rest of my life making it up to both of you."

MJ felt she was living in a dream come true. "What happened?"

"There's no excuse for it," her father said, "but I can try to explain. I let myself get rundown, physically and emotionally, and when Ginger came along, I fell into a fantasy. With you here and your mother in Asheville, I had no one to pull me back to earth."

"Until Grant's party," her mother said.

"One look at your mother," her father continued, gazing at Cat with such devotion it brought tears to MJ's eyes, "and I realized I had made the biggest mistake of my life. I'd traded something real and precious for a few cheap thrills. I can't tell you how sorry I am."

"Jim took Ginger home that night," Cat said, "and left her immediately. He was waiting for me at my

Asheville apartment when I returned from your nana's."

Her father's contrite expression warmed MJ's heart. "I begged your mother's forgiveness and asked her to give me another chance."

MJ looked from one parent to another. "So everything's all right?"

Her mother took her hands and squeezed them. "Not yet. Not totally. But it will be."

"We're seeing a marriage counselor," her father said. "I'm trying to understand what happened to make damned sure it never happens again. And the counselor's helping me deal with my guilt over the pain I've caused my family."

"And," her mother added, "helping me handle my anger."

MJ shook her head. "But how, after all that happened…"

Her mother's smile was radiant. "How can we still be together? The bigger question is how can we not?"

"I've spent the happiest years of my life with your mother," Jim said. "And I hope to spend the rest of my life with her."

"Now," her mother said, "before you clean up, tell your father where to make dinner reservations."

MJ's heart sang all the way to the shower.

GRANT STUMBLED with weariness as he walked in the door. The past three weeks had seemed like years, a blur of disappointment, hard work and lonely nights when he'd been too exhausted to suffer the depths of his loss for long before falling asleep. And too tired to dwell on the anger that consumed him. He'd learned to live without Merrilee until she'd waltzed back into his life last month. Relearning that skill was even more difficult the second time around.

He'd awakened the morning after Merrilee's birthday dinner and reached for her, only to find her gone. Downstairs he'd discovered a note, short but to the point.

"Grant," she'd written, "thank you for everything. I've called Brynn to take me home. My plane leaves in the morning. I don't know when, or if, I'll be back in Pleasant Valley. Please don't try to contact me. My mind is made up. I'm sorry. MJ."

In spite of her request, he'd tried calling her home, but no one answered. The same at her grandmother's. He'd thought of driving to the airport to intercept her, but discarded the idea. He shouldn't have forced her to make love with him, even though he'd sensed she'd wanted it as much as he did. He'd hoped their lovemaking would change her mind about leaving. But if the love they'd shared that night hadn't kept her with him, nothing he could have said the next morning would have changed her mind.

He'd berated himself for pushing her too far too fast. Then he'd finally accepted that her mind had been made up and her flight booked long before he'd taken her to his bed.

When he'd arrived late at the clinic that morning, Fran had greeted him with a puzzled expression. "Jim left a voice mail message. Said he's taking off for a few weeks and wants you to cover for him. What's going on?"

"Damned if I know." His guess was that Jim had gone away with Ginger. "Good thing that new vet's on board in Walhalla. I'll be putting in overtime as it is."

But he'd been thankful for the extra workload in the long run. Keeping busy had kept him sane, kept him from dwelling on the questions that swarmed him like killer bees, alighting to sting every now and then. What more could he have done to ease Merrilee's fears? How could he have kept her with him? Had he only imagined their lovemaking had been as special to her as it had to him? And what had happened to Jim? Was he still with Ginger? And how was Cat faring? Not a breath of gossip had circulated in town since the dinner party at Grant's. Even Jodie, his usual source of information, could tell him nothing.

Without appetite but needing his strength to keep the practice going, he was heating leftovers in the microwave when the phone rang. He didn't dare hope it might be Merrilee, but nonetheless, he felt breathless with anticipation when he answered.

"Hey, Grant. It's Brynn. Hope I'm not calling too late."

Disappointment rolled through him. "No, I just got in."

"Any word from Merrilee?"

"Why would she contact me?" He didn't try to hide his bitterness.

"I'm calling about that other matter you wanted me to check into."

Grant drew a blank.

"The phone threats Merrilee received," Brynn reminded him.

"Moot point now, aren't they?"

"Not exactly."

Grant's pulse revved. "You don't think she's in danger?"

"Not anymore." Brynn's satisfied chuckle sounded through the wire. "Not since I gave the culprit a good chewing out."

"Who was it? Ginger Parker?"

"Closer to home. Your niece."

"Brittany?" Grant shook his head in disbelief. "Why would Brittany threaten Merrilee?"

"She also flattened her tires. Seems your niece didn't take too kindly to Merrilee's breaking her favorite uncle's heart."

"My heart's not broken," he lied. "I hope you straightened Brittany out."

"She'll walk the line. For a while." Brynn sighed. "Jodie has her hands full with that one. By the way, have you heard from Jim?"

"Not since his message saying he was taking time off. I'm hoping he'll be back soon. Have you heard anything?"

"Not from the Strattons," Brynn said. "Cat may be back in Asheville. The good news is there's a For Sale sign in Ginger Parker's front yard and no one's seen her for weeks."

"I no longer have a stake in Stratton family business," Grant assured her, "except in getting my partner back to work so I can get some rest."

"It's late," Brynn said. "I'll let you go."

"Thanks for the info on Brittany. I'll keep a closer eye on her."

"No problem. See you around."

Poor Jodie, he thought. Brittany was growing more problematic every day. He'd have a talk with his sister to ask how he could help his niece's rebelliousness, if he could find a spare minute.

The microwave had dinged during his conversation with Brynn. Grant removed his plate and took it and Gloria's kibble into the living room in front of the fireplace. Days were growing longer and warmer with spring in full bud. Soon it would be too hot for fires.

Grant stared at the flames as he ate, trying to block images of Merrilee from his mind. When that proved futile, he planned a raid on New York in which he'd kidnap Merrilee and bring her home. Home to him and this house.

You're fantasizing, he warned himself. *Look where that kind of thinking landed Jim Stratton. Besides, even*

*if you could drag Merrilee back here, what would you
do? Chain her to the wall to make her stay?*

Disgusted with his thoughts, he carried his plate to
the dishwasher and returned to the sofa. He'd slept
there the last three weeks, unable to endure his bed
with its memories of Merrilee and her honeysuckle fragrance still clinging to the sheets.

He was reaching to turn out the light when the doorbell rang. Gloria lifted her head and barked softly.

"Easy, girl. It's probably Brynn, working the night
shift and wanting to talk more about Brittany."

He considered not answering. In his present state of
mind, he wasn't fit company for man nor beast. As he
hesitated, a car pulled away.

Good, he thought. *Now I can try to sleep.*

To his surprise, the doorbell sounded again.

He pushed to his feet and plodded wearily to the
door. When he opened it, his weariness evaporated in
astonishment. "Merrilee?"

In the yellow glow of the porch light, she resembled
a golden dream, her pale blond hair curling around her
heart-shaped face, blue eyes shining, her cheeks flushed
with a delightful rosy glow. For a moment Grant wondered if he'd fallen asleep after all. Her luggage sat at
her feet and the smile she gave him was tentative, tinged
with fear.

"How'd you get here?" he asked.

"Dad dropped me off. Can I come in?"

He held himself back from scooping her into his arms. She'd burned him twice. Was he crazy enough to be burned again? "On your way to a shoot somewhere?"

Her cheeks flushed deeper red and she shook her head. "I don't blame you for being angry. I've been such a fool."

Dazed, he couldn't believe what he was hearing.

Her eyes pleaded with him. "I've come home, Grant, if you'll have me."

"Home?" He still couldn't wrap his mind around the fact that she was actually standing on his front porch.

She nodded, eyes shining. "Home to you. Home to stay."

With a groan of happiness, he reached for her, lifted her off her feet and crushed her to him. "I thought I'd lost you forever."

He kissed her then, like a thirsty man gulping water, as if he could never get enough. She clasped her arms around his neck and held on tight. When he finally came up for air, he set her on her feet and grabbed her bags. "Come in. It's cold and damp out."

Merrilee stepped inside. With a howl of delight, Gloria lunged at her, placed her front paws on her shoulders and licked her cheek. Merrilee buried her face in the dog's fur.

"Hey, girl," she murmured. "I've missed you, too."

Grant placed her luggage inside the door, closed it and followed Merrilee to the sofa. With the first shock of her arrival wearing off, his caution returned.

"What changed your mind?" he asked.

"Mom and Dad." She settled in the corner and patted the seat for him to sit beside her. "They came to New York."

"Together? That's good news."

So that's where Jim had been while Grant had been working his butt off. But since his partner's trip had resulted in Merrilee's return, Grant considered three weeks of hard labor well worth it.

Merrilee's blue eyes sparkled with happiness. "Your dinner party did the trick. Dad took Ginger home that night and hasn't seen her since. Brynn was right. Seeing Mom and me in the same room with Ginger was the ultimate reality check. It snapped Dad out of his fantasy like a dash of icy water."

"And your mom? She's okay with taking him back?"

Merrilee's expression dimmed. "They're having some rough spots. Who wouldn't under the circumstances? But they're seeing a marriage counselor in Greenville three times a week."

"But you said they were in New York?"

Merrilee nodded. "They flew up for the day to talk to me."

"About their reunion?"

She shook her head. "About us."

He bit his tongue to keep from reminding her the last time he'd seen her she'd insisted there hadn't been an "us."

"What about your career?" He needed assurance on that obstacle first.

The excitement in her face lit up the room. "My agent has an offer on my book from a publisher. And, as you always said, I can take pictures anywhere."

The knot of apprehension eased in his stomach. "You said your parents came to New York to talk about us. What did they say?"

Merrilee reached for his hand. "They know I love you. And I've always known I love you."

Somehow he'd always known, too. "But you were afraid."

She stroked his cheek with her other hand. "Afraid it wouldn't last. Afraid of being devastated when it didn't. I thought we had too many differences for the long haul."

"You were using your parents' marriage as a yard-stick."

Merrilee nodded. "But I didn't have the whole picture. I believed they'd never argued because they never fought in front of me. And I thought they'd always agreed on everything. What I didn't realize was how well they'd learned to compromise."

"And Ginger? Your dad's affair hasn't scared you off for good?"

She shook her head. "Mom and Dad made the trip especially to convince me that when love is real, it can overcome any obstacles." Her eyes clouded. "I guess that's what I'm here to find out."

He felt a sudden catch in his chest. "Whether your love for me is real."

She laughed. "Lordy, no. I know that as sure as I know the sun will rise tomorrow." She grew quiet for a second before saying softly, "I need to know whether I've killed your love for me with all my fears and running away."

He was drowning in emotions: love, relief, joy so intense he couldn't speak. He rose from the sofa and crossed the room to a desk on the other side. From its top drawer, he removed a tiny box and returned to Merrilee's side.

Anxiety had created a crease between her feathery brows. "Do you still love me, Grant?"

He popped open the box and withdrew the aquamarine circled with diamonds. "I've always loved you, Merrilee. That's why I've held on to this, hoping against hope you'd wear it again someday."

Tears glistened in her eyes. "Oh, Grant. The sky and the stars, just like you promised."

He slid the ring on her finger. "Will a June wedding suit you?"

Merrilee threw her arms around his neck. Her lips brushed his ear. "Two whole months? If I can wait that long."

"I love you, Merrilee June."

"And I love you. No more running away from that fact."

Grant hugged her to him. He was the luckiest man

on the planet. With Merrilee at his side, Pleasant Valley had become almost heaven, as close to paradise on earth as a man could get.

* * * * *

Don't miss ONE GOOD MAN, the next book in
Charlotte Douglas' brand-new miniseries,
A PLACE TO CALL HOME,
coming in January 2005,
only from Harlequin American Romance.

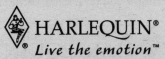

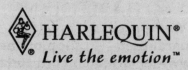

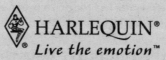